<u>What Kids Say About Carole Marsh Mysteries . . .</u>

I love the real locations! Reading the book always makes me want to go and visit them all on our next family vacation. My Mom says maybe, but I can't wait!

One day, I want to be a real kid in one of Ms. Marsh's mystery books. I think it would be fun, and I think I am a real character anyway. I filled out the application and sent it in and am keeping my fingers crossed!

History was not my favorite subject till I starting reading Carole Marsh Mysteries. Ms. Marsh really brings history to life. Also, she leaves room for the scary and fun.

I think Christina is so smart and brave. She is lucky to be in the mystery books because she gets to go to a lot of places. I always wonder just how much of the book is true and what is made up. Trying to figure that out is fun!

Grant is cool and funny! He makes me laugh a lot!!

I like that there are boys and girls in the story of different ages. Some mysteries I outgrow, but I can always find a favorite character to identify with in these books.

They are scary, but not too scary. They are funny. I learn a lot. There is always food which makes me hungry. I feel like I am there.

What Adults Say About Carole Marsh Mysteries . . .

I think kids love these books because they have such a wealth of detail. I know I learn a lot reading them! It's an engaging way to look at the history of any place or event. I always say I'm only going to read one chapter to the kids, but that never happens—it's always two or three, at least! —Librarian

Reading the mystery and going on the field trip—Scavenger Hunt in hand—was the most fun our class ever had! It really brought the place and its history to life. They loved the real kids characters and all the humor. I loved seeing them learn that reading is an experience to enjoy! —4th grade teacher

Carole Marsh is really on to something with these unique mysteries. They are so clever; kids want to read them all. The Teacher's Guides are chock full of activities, recipes, and additional fascinating information. My kids thought I was an expert on the subject—and with this tool, I felt like it! —3rd grade teacher

My students loved writing their own Real Kids/Real Places mystery book! Ms. Marsh's reproducible guidelines are a real jewel. They learned about copyright and more & ended up with their own book they were so proud of! —Reading/Writing Teacher

The Mystery at
DISNEY WORLD

by
Carole Marsh

Editorial Assistant: Amanda McCutcheon

Cover design: Steve St. Laurent; Editor: Jenny Corsey; Graphic Design: Steve St. Laurent; Layout and footer design: Lynette Rowe; Photography: Amanda McCutcheon.

Also available:
The Mystery at Disney World Teacher's Guide
1,000 Readers - Walt Disney: Master of Imagination

This book is dedicated to Lindsay, a very special girl who deserves the world.
– *AM*

This book is a complete work of fiction. All events are fictionalized, and although the first names of real children are used, their characterization in this book is fiction.

For additional information on Carole Marsh Mysteries, visit: www.carolemarshmysteries.com

Gallopade is proud to be a member and supporter of these educational organizations and associations:

International Reading Association
National Association for Gifted Children
The National School Supply and Equipment Association
Association for Supervision and Curriculum Development
The National Council for the Social Studies
Museum Store Association
Association of Partners for Public Lands
American Library Association

NSSEA

ASCD

A day at Disney!

20 YEARS AGO . . .

As a mother and an author, one of the fondest periods of my life was when I decided to write mystery books for children. At this time (1979) kids were pretty much glued to the TV, something parents and teachers complained about the way they do about video games today.

I decided to set each mystery in a real place—a place kids could go and visit for themselves after reading the book. And I also used real children as characters. Usually a couple of my own children served as characters, and I had no trouble recruiting kids from the book's location to also be characters.

Also, I wanted all the kids—boys and girls of all ages—to participate in solving the mystery. And, I wanted kids to learn something as they read. Something about the history of the location. And I wanted the stories to be funny.

That formula of real+scary+smart+fun served me well. The kids and I had a great time visiting each site and many of the events in the stories actually came out of our experiences there. (For example, we really did have some wild and crazy adventures at Disney World!)

I love getting letters from teachers and parents who say they read the book with their class or child, then visited the historic site and saw all the places in the mystery for themselves. What's so great about that? What's great is that you and your children have an experience that bonds you together forever. Something you shared. Something you both cared about at the time. Something that crossed all age levels—a good story, a good scare, a good laugh!

20 years later,

Carole Marsh

Christina Yother   **Grant Yother**   **Sarah Burney**   **Stuart Coburn**

About the Characters

Christina Yother, 9, from Peachtree City, Georgia

Grant Yother, 7, from Peachtree City, Georgia
Christina's brother

Sarah Burney, 9, as Crystal Jerome, 11, from Orlando,
    Florida

Stuart Coburn, as Mick Jerome, 13, Crystal's brother,
    also from Orlando, Florida

The many places featured in the book actually exist and are
worth a visit! Perhaps you could read the book and see some of
the places the kids visited during their mysterious adventure!

Titles in the Carole Marsh Mysteries Series

Books and Teacher's Guides are available at booksellers, libraries, school supply stores, museums, and many other locations!

CONTENTS

1 WE'RE GOING TO DISNEY WORLD!

"I'm going to Disneyland!" shouted Grant, jumping up and down on Christina's bed. This wasn't her brother's first trip to Disney, but he sure acted like it, his sister Christina thought.

"Grant!" she cried. "It's 5 a.m.! Go back to sleep. The park doesn't open for another four hours!" When Grant didn't stop bouncing up and down, Christina threw her pillow at Grant and knocked him down. "Go back to bed!"

Grant hopped off of Christina's bed, stuck his tongue out at his sister, and headed straight for Mimi and Papa's room in their condominium. He didn't care if the park didn't open for another *24 hours*, he wanted to be first in line. Much to Grant's surprise, Papa was sitting at the table in the kitchen reading the morning paper.

"Good morning, kiddo!" Papa said, as he sipped his

Grant!

It's 5 AM!

cup of coffee.

"I'm going to Disneyland!" shouted Grant again.

Papa laughed and said, "Actually, you are going to Disney World. Disneyland is in Anaheim, California, and we are in Orlando, Florida."

"Oh," Grant said. "I'm going to Disney World!"

Papa just smiled and went back to reading his *Orlando Sentinel*. Christina came out of the bedroom stretching and yawning. She was just as excited about being in Orlando as Grant was. When Mimi and Papa invited Grant and Christina to go to Disney World, Christina could hardly wait. She knew that Mimi had never been to Disney World. And since Christina had been many times before—Papa called her a seasoned pro—she planned to show Mimi the ropes!

"Morning, Papa," she said, as she headed into the kitchen. Grabbing her favorite cereal, a carton of milk, and two bowls and spoons, Christina joined Grant and Papa at the table. She knew that between writing a mystery and visiting Disney World, Mimi was going to have a busy day, so she fixed breakfast for herself and Grant while Mimi slept in.

"Morning, princess," Papa said, as he finished his paper. Papa woke up early every morning—even when they were on vacation—to walk a few miles, and read the morning paper. "How did you sleep?"

It's 5 AM!

Morning, Papa!

"I couldn't go to sleep!" interrupted Grant. "I didn't sleep a wink!"

"Oh, and I suppose that's why you woke me up five times with your snoring last night," Christina teased.

"Did not!" Grant protested.

"Did too!" Christina shrieked.

"Did not!" Grant shouted again.

"All right, all right you two!" Papa said, as he finished his cup of coffee. "Grant, why don't you go get the map of the park, so we can plot our adventure for today!"

Papa always knew how to stop Christina and Grant from arguing.

Grant quickly ran into their bedroom to get the Magic Kingdom map that the people at Disney had sent to Mimi for her book research. Christina cleared their cereal bowls and Papa's coffee cup, and put them into the dishwasher.

When she returned to the table, Papa had already spread out the colorful map for them all to see.

"So, Christina, where do you want to go first?" Papa asked.

With no hesitation at all, Christina answered, "Tomorrowland! Space Mountain is my favorite roller coaster ever!"

"Well, I want to go to Frontierland!" insisted Grant.

Morning, Papa

Plotting Our
Adventure

"Big Mountain Railroad Thunder is *my* favorite roller coaster ever!"

"Grant! It's the Big Thunder Mountain Railroad, silly." Christina laughed.

"That's what I said, Christina. The Big Mountain Railroad Thunder."

This time, Christina didn't even attempt to correct him.

"And look," Grant boasted. "I even brought my coonskin cap that I got in San Antonio at the Alamo." Grant grinned as he put the hat on backwards so that the tail went right down the middle of his face.

"Oh, Grant! You are so silly!" Christina giggled.

"Well kids, we have all day, so don't worry, we'll make it to both attractions," Mimi said, as she joined them at the table.

"I'm sorry Mimi! Did we wake you up?" Christina said. "I told Grant not to be so loud."

"Oh, it's alright. We have a lot of planning to do and I want to be a part of it!"

Mimi always woke up in a great mood, Christina thought. Unlike Mimi, Christina didn't like getting up in the morning, especially when Grant would jump on her bed and scream at the top of his lungs. Being a human alarm clock

Plotting Our
Adventure

Where To
Go First

was his favorite way to wake his sleeping sister.

"Alright, so let's make a plan!" Mimi said, her pad and pencil in hand. Christina didn't remember ever seeing her grandmother without something to write on. Usually, it was her laptop computer. But, she decided lugging a laptop around the nearly 30,000 acres of Disney World didn't sound like too much fun, so she opted for the old-fashioned way— pencil and paper.

"There are six *lands* in Disney World: Adventureland, Frontierland, Fantasyland, Tomorrowland, Mickey's Toontown Fair, and Liberty Square," said Mimi.

"Mickey's Toontown Fair and Liberty Square aren't *lands*, Mimi!" Grant laughed. He loved when he knew something the adults didn't.

"Well, although they don't have *land* in their names, that's what Walt Disney called them," Mimi corrected.

"But first you have to go through Main Street, U.S.A," stated Christina very matter-of-factly.

"Very good, Christina," Papa said. Although he liked to help plan their trips, Christina knew that whatever Mimi wanted to do was what Papa wanted to do. "So where to first?"

"I know, I know!" Grant said, squirming in his seat. "Frontierland!"

Where To
Go First

Let's Make
A Plan!

"Well, I have an idea," said Mimi. "Why don't we go clockwise? We'll start here at Adventureland," she said as she pointed to the map, "and we'll work our way all the way around to Tomorrowland."

Christina knew that Mimi was being diplomatic. If she went counterclockwise, they would start with Christina's favorite–Tomorrowland, and Grant wouldn't be very happy about that. With Mimi's plan, they wouldn't start with anyone's favorite. And secretly she hoped that Grant would be so tired by the time they made it to Tomorrowland that he wouldn't want to ride Space Mountain with her.

"Sounds great to me!" said Grant.

"Sounds wonderful to me!" Papa agreed.

"Sounds perfect to me!" Christina said, with a laugh.

"Then we are agreed!" Mimi smiled.

All of a sudden Mimi jumped up from the table with a panicked look on her face and said, "Oh my goodness!"

"What's the matter, Mimi?" Christina said worriedly. "Did you forget something?"

"Oh, no!" Mimi gasped.

"What, *what*?" Grant insisted.

"Just look at the clock!" Mimi cried.

Let's Make
A Plan!

Look At
The Clock!

2 WHERE ARE THE TICKETS?

"It's already seven o'clock! We're going to be late!" Mimi shouted. Although their condo was only a few minutes from Disney World, Christina knew that like Grant, Mimi wanted to be first in line.

All at once, Grant, Christina, Papa, and Mimi rushed to their rooms to get dressed. Grant and Christina took turns brushing their teeth and washing their faces, while Papa helped Mimi gather all of her research. Within ten minutes the whole crew was lined up at the door ready to go.

Papa began to rattle off his checklist.

"Camera?"

"Check!" Mimi said.

"Watches?"

"Check!" they said, as they looked at their Carole

Look At
The Clock!

Checklist

Marsh Mysteries Fan Club watches.

"Maps?"

"Check!" Grant said, holding up his handful of different maps.

"Sunblock?"

"Check!" Christina said, a smudge of white cream glistening on the tip of her nose.

"Tickets?" Papa finished, but nobody answered.

"*Tickets*?" he repeated.

Christina looked at Papa and giggled.

"Papa, *you* have the tickets!" she said.

"Oh, that's right! I almost forgot!" Papa reached into his front pocket and pulled out their tickets. "Check."

"Then, let's go!" Mimi cheered.

But before Papa's hand reached the doorknob, someone knocked on the door.

"Who is it?" Grant asked.

"It's a surprise!" a voice said from the other side of the door. Mimi looked at Papa with a puzzled look. Christina could tell they didn't know who it was either.

Papa opened the door, and standing on the other side were two kids that Christina had never seen before.

"Hi!" the boy said. "My name is Mick." Christina thought he looked like he was about 13 years old, and he

Checklist   A Surprise?

was kind of cute. "And this is my little sister, Crystal."

"Hi!" Crystal smiled at Christina. "And I'm not little, I'm 11 years old!" she said as she glared at her older brother. "We're here to give you a personal tour of Disney World!"

"You must be Grant and Christina," Mick said, as he shook Grant's hand.

"Sure am! And this is Mimi and Papa," Grant said, pointing to his grandparents.

"Pleased to meet you," Mick said.

"Wow, we've never had a personal tour before. And we've been here lots of times!" Christina said.

"Well, when Mimi called Disney to talk about writing her mystery, she spoke with a friend of our Dad," Mick told them.

"Mr. Rupert?" Mimi guessed.

"Yes ma'am," said Crystal. "Our father is friends with Mr. Rupert. He's a Disney Imagineer."

"Imagin—who?" questioned Grant.

"Imagineer. That's what Mr. Disney called the original architects and planners of Disneyland. Today, Imagineers are all the people who create audio-animatronic figures, special effects, ride systems, show controls, and so forth at Disney," Mick explained.

A Surprise?

Meet Mick & Crystal

"Anima—what?" Grant asked.

"Audio-animatronic figures are mechanized puppets that can be preprogrammed or controlled with a remote," Mick answered. "But we are getting way ahead of ourselves. Why don't we head to the park and Crystal and I will tell you a lot more."

Mick and Crystal led Mimi, Papa, Grant, and Christina down the stairs of the condo to an official Walt Disney World bus that was waiting for them.

"Wow," Papa said, "we really are getting the star treatment aren't we?"

"Well, it's not every day that our favorite author comes to visit," Crystal said, as they found their seats and buckled seatbelts.

"I want to sit up front with the driver!" insisted Grant.

Christina gave him a look and said, "You know you aren't allowed to ride in the front seat, Grant."

"But . . ." Grant began to whine.

Before he could finish, Mick said, "You don't want to sit up front, little buddy. You won't be able to hear us finish the story."

Christina knew Mick knew Grant wasn't allowed to sit up front, but he was just trying to be nice.

Meet Mick
& Crystal

Our Own
Bus!

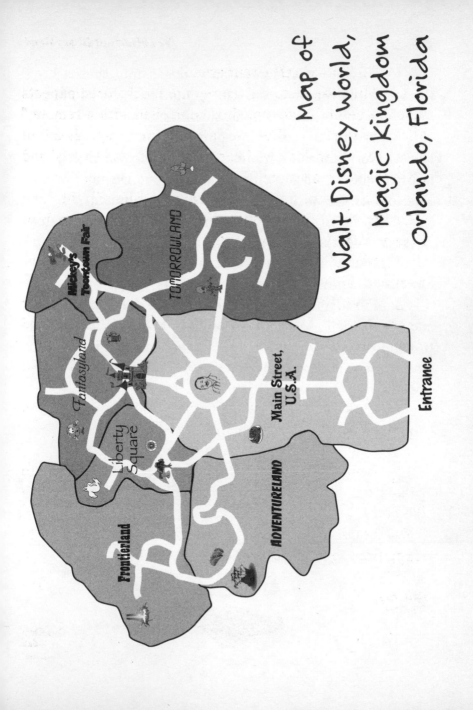

Map of
Walt Disney World,
Magic Kingdom
Orlando, Florida

"Okay!" Grant agreed and settled into the back of the bus with everyone else. He seemed to really like Mick. As soon as he buckled up, they were on their way.

"As Crystal was saying, our father is an Imagineer at Disney World too. His friend Mr. Rupert told him that our favorite author was writing a book about Disney. When Dad told us, we were so excited!" Mick continued.

"It was my idea to give you a personal tour," boasted Crystal. "We thought it might be fun for you too!"

Mimi smiled, "Well, we are honored. It's not every day that you get a tour from the experts, right?"

"Exactly! Plus, we really wanted to meet you, Grant and Christina," Mick said, smiling at Christina. She thought to herself that Mick was *really* cute. "I think we'll have a really good time."

Our
Own Bus!

A Personal
Tour Too!

3 JUST LIKE WALT

"Mimi," Grant said, "tell us the story of Walt Disney again!"

"But you've heard it a million times Grant," Mimi said with a smile. "Are you sure you want to hear it again?"

"Please!" Grant begged.

"Okay. That is if it is alright with Crystal and Mick," she said.

"Oh, please do!" Crystal exclaimed.

"As you know Grant, Walt Disney is one of my favorite people," Mimi began.

"Why is that?" Mick asked.

"Well, a lot of people think that Walt Disney must have had a super fun life. You know, because he was so creative and innovative. But actually, Mr. Disney's childhood was not all that easy," Mimi began.

A Personal Tour Too!

Walt's Story

13

"He was born on December 5, 1901. His family said his Dad had 'ants in his pants' because he never liked to stay in the same place for too long. So that meant that Walt had to move from place to place many times when he was growing up," Mimi continued.

"When Walt was only five years old, his Dad bought a farm with cows, pigs, chickens, ducks, and two large apple orchards. Each of his kids—including Walt—had certain responsibilities on the farm.

"Walt's job was to take care of the pigs. He had a favorite called Porky who would come up to the house and push her little snout up against Walt's window. He also named many of the other animals on the farm."

"But when did he start drawing cartoons?" Grant asked.

"One day Walt took a brush and painted yucky, black tar on the walls of his house," Mimi said. "Needless to say, his Dad wasn't very happy about that. But his aunt gave Walt paper and pencil so that he could keep drawing.

"When he was only seven years old, Walt was commissioned by a family friend to draw a portrait of a horse named Rupert. He was paid a nickel for the drawing."

"He must not have been a very good artist!"

Walt's Story

Child Artist

Christina said.

"Actually he was *really* good," Mimi answered. "Back in 1908 a nickel was a lot of money for a seven-year-old boy."

"Oh," Christina said, thinking that wouldn't go far for a kid's allowance these days.

"Times were tough for Walt's parents, and his father decided to move the family back to the city. This time they went to Kansas City," Mimi continued.

"Walt convinced his Dad to let him take an art class at the Kansas City Art Institute. He made lots of friends while he was there. He and a friend started entering talent contests with their jokes, and even won some! In one act, Walt pretended to be a photographer taking pictures. He used a fake camera that squirted people in the face when he took a picture, or a bird would fly out of a hole in the camera."

"Wow," Grant marveled, "I want to do that. That would be so much fun!"

"Walt always found a way to have fun when he was young. He wasn't as lucky as you Grant," Mimi said. "He didn't have all the cool toys like you do. So he created many of his own."

"That's called ingenuity, Grant," Papa added.

Child Artist

Ingenuity!

"Engine—what?" Grant asked.

"In—ja—noo—eh—ty," Papa pronounced for Grant. "It means he was very clever and creative."

"Oh," Grant said. "That's cool."

"Yes," Mimi agreed. "Walt was pretty cool. He helped his family by delivering papers before and after school. When he was 17, his parents moved the family to Chicago. But Walt really liked Kansas City, so he stayed for the summer, then joined his family that fall.

"Walt even became the art editor of the McKinley High School newspaper. It was his first step in becoming a serious artist. He had his own little section of the paper that he would fill with patriotic cartoons in support of World War I. Walt was so patriotic, that he even lied about his age so he could join the Red Cross a year early!

"When Walt returned home from working for the Red Cross in France, his Dad had found him a job as the head of a jelly factory. It paid $25 a week!" Mimi said.

"So did he take it?" Crystal asked. She had never heard this part of the story before.

"Nope!" Mimi said. "He moved to Kansas City instead and found a job working as an assistant for two commercial artists. And there he made a lifelong friend named Ub Iwerks."

Ingenuity !

Back To
Kansas City

"Ub-what?" asked Grant.

"Ub Iwerks," Mimi repeated. "It's a real name."

"It's a real funny name," Grant said, but the others just ignored him.

"Walt didn't work there for very long," Mimi continued. "They didn't have enough work for him or his friend, Mr. Iwerks, so the pair started their own business designing flyers and advertisements for different companies. Then the two men both took jobs at the Kansas City Film Ad Company, and that's where Walt first worked with animation," Mimi said.

"Too cool!" Grant cheered.

"Walt created cartoons for other people for a long time. He was one of the first people to use 'cels' for his cartoons," Mimi said.

"What are 'cels'?" Christina asked.

"The word 'cel' is short for celluloid, which is a transparent sheet that artists paint on. An artist uses one 'cel' to paint the background of a cartoon, and then more 'cels' are used to paint characters in motion. This way they don't have to repaint the background over and over again," Mimi explained.

"But when the company didn't have enough work for Walt, he decided to leave Missouri. In July of 1923, Walt

Back To
Kansas City

Artist At
Work

boarded the California Limited train with only one shirt and change of underwear, and a head full of ideas. At first, he tried to get a job as a movie director in Hollywood, but the answer he got everywhere he went was 'No opening!'" Mimi continued.

"Believing he had nothing to lose, Walt decided to send one of his *Alice in Cartoonland* films to an important cartoon distributor in New York. She loved it so much that she asked Walt for six more! Walt then asked his brother Roy to handle the business end of their new company, the Disney Brothers Studio. Today, it has been renamed The Walt Disney Studio.

"One day, the distributor in New York suggested that Walt create a series with a rabbit hero," Mimi explained. "Walt worked extra hard to create his new character *Oswald*, who became a very popular cartoon. But then the distributor surprised Walt by offering him a lot less money for new cartoons then he was already getting paid. He told Walt that he would put him out of business if he didn't agree. And since the distributor owned the rights to *Oswald*, Walt couldn't fight back. That day, Walt vowed never to work for anyone else ever again," Mimi said.

"That's so sad!" Christina said.

"Well, on a train on his way back to Hollywood, Walt

Artist At Work

Films &
Movies

created an even more famous character than *Oswald*. Walt created Mickey Mouse," Mimi explained.

"Does that mean that Mickey Mouse was born on a train?" Grant asked.

"Well, I guess it does," Mimi laughed. *"Steamboat Willie* was the first cartoon featuring Mickey Mouse. It was also Walt's first 'talking film,'" Mimi continued. "Film producers loved *Steamboat Willie* so much that they wanted to hire Walt to make the cartoon for them. But, remembering his vow to never work for anyone else again, Walt said thanks, but no thanks.

"Mickey Mouse became popular during the Great Depression, because he was able to cheer everyone up. Mickey Mouse made Walt's company more successful. His other cartoons included *Silly Symphonies, Flowers and Trees,* and *The Three Little Pigs.* His first full length movie was *Snow White and the Seven Dwarfs,*" Mimi said.

"That's one of my favorites!" Crystal proclaimed.

"Mine too!" Christina added.

"Well," Mimi said, "it almost didn't get made!"

"Really?" Crystal asked. "Why not?"

"It cost more than a million dollars to make that kind of movie back then. But thanks to Walt's older brother Roy, they were able to borrow the money from the Bank of

films & Movies

Mickey Mouse!

America," Mimi answered.

"After his Disney Studios took off, Walt decided he wanted to build a theme park too. He didn't like taking his daughters to any other theme parks because they were always so dirty," Mimi said.

"That's what I love about Disney World," Mick added. "It's always so clean and litter-free."

"After working out a deal with the American Broadcasting Company, Walt was given the money to build his theme park," Mimi said, "and the rest is history!"

Mickey Mouse!

Theme Parks

4 KNOW YOUR PARKS

Just as Mimi finished her story, they drove up to the gates leading into Walt Disney World. A big WELCOME TO WALT DISNEY WORLD sign greeted them. Goosebumps of anticipation popped up on Christina's arms. Every time she came to Disney World, she got more and more excited. Because they were in an official bus, they didn't have to wait in the long line of cars and vans entering the park.

"Wow," Grant marveled. "We're going to be in the front of the line!"

Ignoring Grant, Christina got Mick's attention and asked, "How did your father get such a cool job as an Imagineer?"

Mick answered, "To make a long story short, our grandfather was one of Mr. Disney's original Imagineers. He worked at the Disney Studio before Disneyland was

Theme Parks

We're Here!

21

even built. Then he traveled around the world visiting different theme parks to collect ideas for Disneyland in California. I guess our Dad took after our grandfather, because after college, he got a job at Disney World, and has worked there ever since!"

"Are you going to be an Imagineer too, Mick?" Christina asked.

"I hope so!" Mick said with a smile.

"Me too!" Crystal chimed in.

"I heard there is an awesome roller coaster called the Rock 'n Roller Coaster at Disney," Papa said. "That sounds like fun."

"No, Papa, that's at MGM Studios." Christina answered.

"What's the difference? Aren't they all the same?" Papa questioned.

"Oh, oh . . . I know this one, I know this one!" Grant chanted, as he squirmed in his seat. "Mimi said that in the Magic Kingdom there are seven 'lands.' But the Magic Kingdom is one of four parks at Disney World. There's also EPCOT, Disney-MGM Studios, and Disney's Animal Kingdom."

"Very good, Grant," Mimi said, giving Grant a high-five.

"There're also two water parks, a sports complex, and a place for one giant block party called Downtown Disney," Mick began. "That's what all those directional signs alongside the road are about. Mr. Disney wanted Disney World to run like its own city. After Disneyland was built, he was unhappy because of all the flashy hotels and cheap kinds of entertainment that sprung up around it. So he bought 30,000 acres of land near Orlando and got permission from the local government to run Disney World like a town."

"And look where it is today!" Papa said, as they pulled up in front of the park.

"This is where we get off," Crystal said.

"Make sure you have everything," Papa reminded them. Everyone looked around to make sure they hadn't left anything on the bus.

"Who's got the tickets?" Papa asked.

"Papa!" the whole group said in unison.

"Just kidding," he laughed.

As they clambered off the bus, Christina couldn't believe how hot it was, and how excited she was. Going to the park with her Mom and Dad when she was little had been fun. And showing her little brother around for the first time when he was just a baby had been fun too. But

Imagineering   WELCOME   Off The Bus

this time, she had a feeling her visit was going to be really special.

There were hundreds of people lining up to buy their tickets. She saw a group of girls wearing very brightly colored print dresses. She heard one of them say they were visiting the United States from Tanzania. Christina knew Tanzania was in Africa because she studied about Mt. Kilimanjaro—which is on the northeastern tip of Tanzania—in school.

Christina also heard a group of grown-ups talking who seemed to have British accents. She saw some people wearing turbans whom she thought were probably Muslim. She had learned a lot about Muslims in one of Mimi's books. Each and every time Christina visited Disney World, she saw someone different.

As they headed toward the gate, Christina remembered the last time she was here, waiting in a long line to get through the first set of gates. But this time, Mick and Crystal were leading them past the lines straight to the Monorail station.

"We could take the ferryboat, but it takes a lot longer," Mick explained.

"I like the Monorail better, too!" Christina added. "It's so much more fun."

Off The Bus

To The Monorail!

"Alright," agreed Mimi. "The Monorail it is."

As they moved with the massive flow of people towards the Monorail, Christina noticed there were a lot more people here than she had ever remembered.

"Is there some kind of special celebration going on today?" Christina asked.

"Actually, yes, there is," Crystal answered. "This is what is called the Disney Magic Music Days."

"What's that?" Christina asked. She loved music!

"Every year around this time, outstanding bands, orchestras, choirs, dance groups, drill teams, and other performers from around the world come to perform at the Walt Disney World Resort," Crystal explained. "Groups perform in the Magic Kingdom, EPCOT, Disney-MGM Studios, and Downtown Disney Marketplace."

"I want to sing, I want to dance!" Grant said, hopping around in a circle doing his imitation of a Celtic dancer.

"Actually, little buddy," Mick began, "you have to be a member of a group and you have to apply way ahead of time to perform. And even then, only a few are picked."

Undaunted, Grant continued his funny circular dance as Papa clapped and stomped to the beat.

Christina suggested, "You could take ballet classes

To The
Monorail!

Magic Music
Days

with me, Grant, and then maybe you'll get picked!"

Grant immediately stopped his "happy dance," as he called it, and stuck out his tongue at her.

"You know boys don't take ballet, Christina," he said.

"I do, Grant," Mick said, much to Christina's surprise. "My football coach told me it would help me as a running back. It makes me more agile."

"Why are we on *this* side, and those people are on *that* side," Grant pondered, watching a group of people standing next to another Monorail track.

"That's because that is a different Monorail," Crystal explained. "That one takes you to EPCOT."

"What's that," Grant asked.

"EPCOT stands for Experimental Prototype Community of Tomorrow," Mick explained.

"Why aren't we going there?" asked Grant.

"We'll go to EPCOT another day, Grant," Papa explained. "Today's the day for the Magic Kingdom!"

"Hey look, the Monorail is here!" Mimi exclaimed, as the train swooshed into the station. One by one Grant, Christina, Crystal, Mick, Mimi, and Papa climbed aboard the Monorail.

"This is just like the MARTA in Atlanta, isn't it?"

Magic Music
Days

Not To
EPCOT

Mimi asked Crystal.

"I've never been to Atlanta," said Crystal, "but I'd like to go someday."

"You can come and visit anytime you want," Christina said. "I'll give you and Mick a personal tour of Atlanta and our hometown, Peachtree City." Deep down inside, Christina was thinking that she especially wanted Mick to come. He was so smart and he always knew just what to say to Grant.

"Thanks, Christina, we may take you up on that someday!" Mick answered with a smile.

"Hold on tight! Here we go!" Papa burst out, as the Monorail left the station.

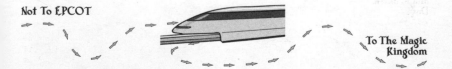

Not To EPCOT

To The Magic Kingdom

5 NO DISNEY WORLD FOR PAPA???

Everyone sat quietly as they watched the magic of Walt Disney World unfold before them. The Monorail was the best way to see Disney World from a distance because it was so high above the ground.

They looked down at all the people riding the ferryboat to the park. Christina thought to herself that she would like to ride the ferryboat when they left the park that night. She got a little sad when she thought of leaving, but as they came around a bend in the track she began to smile again as Cinderella's Castle came into view. That was really her favorite part of the park.

As they zoomed past the lake, they spotted two large hotels in the distance.

"What are those?" Mimi asked Mick.

"The white one over there with the red roof is

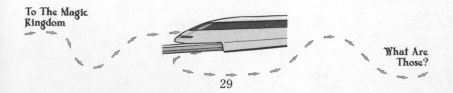

To The Magic
Kingdom

What Are
Those?

Disney's Grand Floridian Resort and Spa," Mick explained. "Our Dad calls it Disney's flagship hotel."

"What's a flagship?" Grant asked.

"A flagship is the main ship. Where the commander stays," Christina explained.

Grant paused for a second. "So that's where Mr. Disney lives?" he asked, looking confused.

"That is one definition of a flagship," Mimi explained. "But I think Mick means the hotel is the most popular at Disney."

"Oh . . . so Mr. Disney doesn't live there?" Grant asked, still confused.

"Actually, Grant, Mr. Disney died more than 30 years ago." Crystal explained. "My grandfather said it was one of the saddest days of his life."

"Oh . . ." Grant said, looking embarrassed.

"Hey Grant," Papa said. "Look at that one over there." Papa motioned towards another hotel that looked like it was taken from the set of the *South Pacific* musical. Papa and Mimi had taken Grant and Christina to see *South Pacific* when the show came to Atlanta.

"Oh, cool!" Grant exclaimed, quickly forgetting his embarrassment.

"That's Disney's Polynesian Resort," Mick

What Are Those?

Resorts!

explained. "It has waterfalls and lots of gardens so that it looks like it's set in the South Seas."

"Let's stay there next time," Christina said to Papa.

"We just might!" Papa said.

As the Monorail zoomed into the station, everyone on the train began to gather their things. As soon as it stopped, one by one they hopped off the train and followed the crowd down to the second set of gates.

"More gates!" Grant cried. "Why are there more gates?"

"This gate is for safety Grant," Christina explained. "This is so no one can bring anything dangerous into the park."

"I guess I can't go in then," Papa interrupted.

"Why is that Papa?" Grant asked.

"Well, my good looks are a dangerous weapon. Women all over the world hurt their necks turning to look at me as I walk by!" Papa said matter-of-factly.

"Oh, Papa," Mimi laughed. "You are so silly!"

"Don't worry, sir," a man wearing a nametag that said JORGE FROM LOS ANGELES, CALIFORNIA. "We'll let you in this time!"

They all burst into laughter.

After Jorge searched Mimi's camera bag and purse,

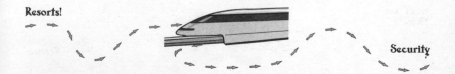

Resorts!

Security

the six adventurers headed for the entrance.

"I've always wondered why the people who work here have different cities on their nametags," Christina said to Crystal.

"That's because it makes people feel more at home here at Disney," she explained. "A lot of people who work here grew up in Orlando, like me. So they have Orlando, Florida on their nametag. But wouldn't it make you feel great to see Peachtree City, Georgia on one?"

"That would be great!" Christina smiled. She wondered what the chances were of that actually happening.

Papa handed each of them their tickets. Mick and Crystal had special passes of their own. Grant's ticket had Goofy printed on the front. Mimi had Minnie Mouse, and Papa had Mickey Mouse. Christina's ticket had Cinderella's Castle on it. Quickly, Grant ran his ticket through the ticket reader and pushed through the turnstile. Then one by one they all walked through.

"I have an idea!" squealed Grant. "Let's take our picture over there in front of the Walt Disney World Railroad and the shrubs and flowers that look like Mickey Mouse."

Everyone agreed as Grant ran toward the wall.

Security

Railroad
Station

After waiting patiently for a few other families to take pictures, Grant climbed up onto the wall.

"Me first! Me first!" he exclaimed.

"Alright," Mimi said, as she fumbled with her camera. "On the count of three. One . . . two . . ." But before she could finish, Grant struck a goofy pose.

"Three!" she said, as she took the picture.

After taking a few more pictures, they walked under the railroad tracks into park.

"Oh, I almost forgot to tell you," Mick said, as they walked past a popcorn vendor. They saw a tall man waving his arms above his head looking directly at them.

"Who's that?" Grant asked.

"That's our Dad. He's going to give Mimi and Papa a special tour," Mick told Grant. "And you and Christina will come with us. If that's okay?"

Mimi did not answer. She was looking around for Papa. She spotted him striking up a conversation with the popcorn vendor.

"Where there's food, Papa's there!" she said to no one in particular.

Railroad
Station

A Special
Adult Tour

6 OVER AND OUT!

After Mimi finally lured Papa away from his new popcorn vendor friend, they handed Grant and Christina each a walkie-talkie.

"Papa and I both have one, too," Mimi said, as Papa showed Grant how to clip his onto his belt. "This way we can all stay in touch with each other, even when we're separated."

"Coooooool!" Grant said, as he fiddled with his blue walkie-talkie.

"Grant!" Christina scolded. "You're gonna break it if you aren't careful." She patted her red walkie-talkie, already clipped onto her belt.

"Now make sure you are tuned to Channel 12," Mimi said.

"When you finish what you are saying to someone

A Special
Adult Tour

Ten-Four,
Over & Out

35

on the walkie-talkie," Papa explained, "you have to say 'Ten-four, over and out.'"

"What does that mean?" Grant asked.

"Ten-four means affirmative, or that you understand what the other person has said. Over and out means that you don't have anything else to say and you will talk to them later," Christina answered.

"Alright," Mick said. "If you guys are ready to go, then let's head out!" Christina was so excited that she was going to spend the whole day with Mick. She had never met a boy who was smarter then she was. Well, other than Papa, of course.

"Don't forget, meet us in front of Cinderella's Castle at 8:30 p.m. so we can watch the fireworks together," Mimi reminded them. After a few hugs and kisses, which Grant tried to wiggle out of, Mimi and Papa headed in the opposite direction with Mick and Crystal's dad, Mr. Jerome.

As soon as the grown-ups walked off, Grant had an idea.

"Why don't we put our walkie-talkies on Channel 13 Christina?" Grant asked. The number 13 always gave Christina the willies. She didn't know why, but it just did. "That way we can talk to each other and not bother Mimi

Ten-Four.
Over & Out

Channel 13

Cool. . . walkie-talkies!

and Papa on their tour."

"That's a good idea Grant," Crystal said. "Our Dad has a lot to show them. And listening to us chatter would only interrupt them." Grant and Christina turned their walkie-talkies up one channel to 13.

"So, where to first?" Mick asked Crystal, their tour guide for the day.

"I thought we could ride on the Walt Disney World Railroad around the park first," Crystal answered.

"Crystal," Mick protested, "I'm sure Christina and Grant have been on the train before. Let's show them something new."

"Alright, Mr. Smarty-Pants," Crystal answered. "Where to first?"

"Let's go to the Pirates of the Caribbean. I want to show them our secret hiding place," Mick smiled.

"Secret hiding place?" Grant asked with a grin.

"Just for you little buddy. We don't take just anyone there. But you and Christina are cool," Mick said, as he smiled at Christina.

"Alright," Crystal agreed. "Pirates of the Caribbean it is. But I want to show them my namesake first."

"Namesake?" Christina asked.

Channel 13

To The Pirates!

"Come on," Crystal said, grabbing Christina's hand. "I'll show you!"

To The Pirates!

And Our
Secret Place

7 A FASTPASS TO WHERE?

Crystal and Christina ran ahead of Mick and Grant past all the fun shops and bakeries on Main Street, U.S.A.

"Yum," Christina said, sniffing the air. "I almost forgot how delectable this place smells. I smell cinnamon rolls and waffle cones! It must be coming from the Main Street Bakery."

"Actually," Crystal said, "that smell is fake!"

"What?" Christina asked in disbelief.

"There are tanks underneath the streets that have the scent in them, and those tanks release wonderful smells!" Crystal explained.

"Really?" Christina asked again. She wondered what other amazing revelations she might learn from her new friends.

Main Street, U.S.A.

Wonderful Smells

"Really!" Mick said. "Come on!"

They took the short cut at Casey's Corner, and ran up to The Crystal Palace.

"This is the Crystal Palace," Crystal explained. "I was named after it."

"It's our Mom's favorite restaurant," Mick said. "She craved this food when she was pregnant with Crystal. She would eat plates of tossed, chicken, and tuna salads. Not to mention bowls upon bowls of soup, hot from the kettle. She loved the spit-roasted carved meats and the fresh pasta. But her favorite was the peel and eat shrimp. And it was all-you-can-eat! She was actually here at the restaurant when she went into labor!"

"That makes me hungry," Grant said rubbing his tummy.

"That's so cool!" Christina exclaimed. "I wish I was named after something at Disney World."

"Hey, come on," Mick said. "Let's go!"

Christina noticed that Mick was anxious to change the topic.

"Aren't you gonna tell them who *you're* named after, *Mick*," Crystal said.

"Oh, oh! I know! I know!" Grant said, as he jumped up and down with his hand above his head. "You were

Wonderful
Smells

The Crystal
Palace

named after Mickey Mouse weren't you!"

It was obvious that Mick wasn't too excited about that.

"Yeah I was," he moped. "I thought it was cool when I was younger."

"I still think it's cool," Christina said, with a smile. Mick gave her a grateful but dubious smile. Christina thought the dimples in his cheeks were so cool.

"Alright, let's go now!" Crystal insisted.

Grant, Christina, Mick, and Crystal took off running. First they crossed a pretty white bridge, and then took a sharp left onto a wooden bridge with a sign overhead that said ADVENTURELAND. Halfway across the bridge, Christina's walkie-talkie slipped off her belt and fell onto the bridge.

When she reached down to pick it up, the walkie-talkie started making noise that sounded like a television when the cable was out. She picked it up, and all of a sudden a voice came over the walkie-talkie singing, *Yo ho! Yo ho! A pirate's life for me!* Christina recognized the song from the Pirates of the Caribbean ride.

Then the voice came over the line again and said, *Follow the pirate rules my friend, or it will be your end!* Christina was stunned.

The Crystal Palace

Adventureland

Pushing the button on the side of the walkie-talkie, Christina demanded, "Who is this?" When she didn't get an answer she repeated, *"Who is this?"*

The same voice came over the line and said, *10–4, over and out!* and then there was nothing but static.

About that time Mick came running back to Christina.

"Come on Christina," he said out of breath. "Catch up!"

But before Christina could tell Mick what she had just heard, he grabbed her hand and pulled her along. She quickly forgot about the sinister message. Surely it wasn't for her, she thought.

When they got to the Pirates of the Caribbean ride, there was already a long, long line.

"We're gonna be in line for half the day!" Christina grumbled.

"Actually," Crystal said, "we don't have to wait in this line. We get to use the Fastpass line."

"What's a Fastpass?" Christina asked.

"All you do is take your admission ticket and stick it into that machine over there. It will give you a Fastpass ticket that tells you what time to come back to the ride so you don't have to wait in line. It usually takes about an

Adventureland

The Pirates!

hour," Mick explained.

"But I don't want to wait an hour," Grant moaned. "I want to go now!"

"Normally, you would have no choice. But today you are lucky," Crystal explained. "Our Dad gave us these special passes that are for unlimited Fastpass access. We don't have to wait to get a Fastpass ticket, we just get in the Fastpass line."

"Wow," Christina exclaimed. "That's like magic!"

"Well . . . what are we waiting for?" Mick said. "Let's go!" The Fastpass line was really short. Christina was excited because she knew that she wouldn't have to wait very long at all.

As they passed through the creepy corridors leading into the Pirates of the Caribbean ride, they saw all kinds of spooky scenes. The walls of rough, gray stone looked like the walls of an old Spanish fort or castle. Around one corner on top of a platform, a cannon pointed out a window.

Grant hopped up onto the platform and mounted the cannon like he was riding a horse. He waved one arm above his head like he was roping cattle and gripped the cannon with his other hand.

"Ride 'em cowboy!" he shouted.

"Grant!" Christina yelled. "Get down from there!"

The Pirates!

Grant!

"Come on little wrangler! You're in Adventureland not Frontierland," Mick said, as he hopped up onto the platform with Grant. "It's more like *Fire in the hole! Aye, aye matey!*" He pretended to shoot a cannon ball from the cannon.

"Alright, boys," Crystal said, as she grew impatient. "Let's go!"

When they approached the boats for the ride, Crystal showed their passes to the man standing at the front of the line. He gave them a boat all to themselves. They each had their own row to sit in.

"Wow," Grant said. "This is too awesome."

"I thought you were going to show us your secret hiding place?" Christina asked Mick.

"Shhhhh," he said. "Not so loud. Otherwise, it won't be a secret anymore."

"Oh, sorry," Christina whispered.

"Just wait," Crystal said. "You'll see!"

Grant!

Secret Hiding
Place

Ride 'em cowboy!

8 AYE AYE, MATEY!

"Before the boat takes off," Christina explained, "we need to assign everyone their pirate duties."

"Ooooh," Crystal cheered. "Like the ones we learned about in *The Mystery of Blackbeard The Pirate* book?"

"Exactly!" Christina continued. "I think since Mick is the oldest, he should be the captain. And he's sitting in the front."

"Well, I'm the next oldest," Crystal said. "So I should be the quartermaster. And Christina, you should be the sailing master."

"What about me?" Grant asked.

"You're the youngest and you're sitting in the back, so you get to be the cabin boy!" Christina giggled, but Grant frowned.

Secret Hiding
Place

Pirate Duties

As the boat began to move forward on the tracks, it made a rumbling noise. A few seconds later, it plopped down into the water with a splash. The fast-moving current tugged them forward on the winding river into the dark cave.

First, the ride took them through a spooky old cave. In the background, Christina heard a voice moan *Dead men tell no tales!"* It gave her the creeps as she passed by the skeletons of pirates. Then suddenly they plummeted down a waterfall.

They landed between a large pirate ship that was firing cannonballs toward a fort wall on the other side of them. Plumes of water sprayed into the air as the cannonballs whizzed past their heads and hit the water.

"Well, since I'm the captain," Mick said, "you have to follow my two rules, the pirate rules. Number one . . . obey all orders, or else!"

"Aye Aye, matey," Crystal said in her best pirate voice.

"Aye Aye, matey," Christina agreed in her best pirate voice.

Grant followed suit, "Aye Aye, matey."

"And number two . . . a pirate who runs away will be marooned!" Mick finished.

Pirate Duties

Pirate Rules

"Aye Aye, matey," Crystal said again in her pirate voice.

"Aye Aye, matey," Christina agreed and waited for Grant to agree. When he didn't, she turned around to the last seat on their boat and realized . . . Grant was gone!

"Grant!" Christina yelped. "Where are you?"

"What's the matter, Christina?" Mick asked.

"Grant's gone! I can't find my little brother!" she cried.

"Where did he go? We're surrounded by water," Crystal said. "It's not like he could have walked away."

"I don't know! Help me find him!" Christina screamed.

Mick climbed over the rows of seats to the back of the boat and asked, "Are you sure he isn't just hiding behind the seat?"

Christina tried to stand up, but the boat rocked. She quickly sat down.

"Be careful, Christina. I don't know how deep the water is," Crystal said.

Mick looked in the back row and could not find Grant. The only thing in the back seat was Grant's blue walkie-talkie.

"Look!" Mick exclaimed, as he showed it to the girls.

Pirate Rules

Where's Grant?

"Isn't this Grant's. . ."

But before he could finish, static spurted out of the walkie-talkie. *Grant's getting soggy just like the rabbit!*

"Who's that?" Crystal asked.

"That's the same voice . . ." Christina began. But then she realized she hadn't told the other kids about the first walkie-talkie message. "The same voice that talked to me on my walkie-talkie on the bridge. It told me to follow the pirate's rules, or it would be my end!"

Christina thought to herself that this was all her fault. If she had just told her friends and little brother what the voice had said, maybe Grant wouldn't be missing!

"What am I going to do?" she cried.

Mick pushed the button on the side of the walkie-talkie to talk.

"Who is this?" he said forcefully. There was no answer.

"If you've done something to my little buddy," Mick began. But his finger slipped off the button before he could finish.

Keep movin', movin', movin', though they're disapprovin'. Keep them dogies movin' . . . the voice said. *10–4, over and out!* And then the static stopped.

"What is he talking about?" Christina asked.

Where's Grant?

Who's That?

"I don't know," Crystal said.

"I never thought I would say this, but I want my brother!" Christina cried.

"Don't worry Christina," Mick said. "We'll find him. He couldn't have gone too far. But there's nothing we can do right now. When the ride is over, we'll find him."

The pirates didn't seem as entertaining without Grant sitting in the back mimicking them. The scenes of the town being attacked by pirates, a man getting dunked in a well, the wench auction were just not as much fun. Crystal and Mick decided they didn't have time to show Christina their secret hiding place, so they just continued on the ride.

At the last scene, the Caribbean town under attack by the pirates was on fire. Christina looked up at two animatronic characters that were tied together on top of a table covered with gold. When she saw the face of one of them, she began to scream.

"What's the matter Christina?" Mick asked.

"Look!" she gasped, as she pointed towards the figures. "Someone put a picture of Grant's face on one of the guys who are tied up! Somebody has taken Grant! Somebody has my little brother!"

Who's That?

Grant's Face

9 LUNCH WITH A PARAKEET?

Christina's stomach began to growl as she sat quietly on the rest of the Pirates of the Caribbean ride. She remembered she didn't eat much of her cereal that morning. And it was just about time for lunch. Poor Grant, she thought. He's probably hungry too.

When the boat finally docked at the end of the ride, Mick helped Crystal and Christina off the boat. The dark tunnel quickly led them out into bright sunlight that made them squint.

"I have an idea," Christina said. "Let's sit down and think this out."

"Why don't we get something to eat while we do that," Mick said. Christina was embarrassed because she thought that maybe he had heard her stomach growling on the ride.

Missing Grant

Something To Eat?

"I'm starved," he added.

Christina sighed in relief.

"That sounds like a good idea to me," she agreed.

"Alright," Crystal said, "then let's go to the *El Pirata Y el Perico Restaurante.* It's right over there."

She pointed to the restaurant.

"What's that mean?" Christina asked.

"It means The Pirate and the Parakeet Restaurant," Mick answered. "They have great tacos and nachos there."

"Okay," Christina agreed. "But we have to make it quick."

Crystal went up to the counter and ordered one large nacho basket, four loaded tacos, and three large drinks. When she returned to the table, Christina and Mick had spread a map of the park over part of the table.

"Here you go, Mick. I got you two tacos since I know you like to eat a lot," Crystal said, with a smile.

"Thanks," he answered.

"I just got two for you and me, Christina. But I thought we could all share the nachos," Crystal said, as she handed Christina a taco and placed the mound of nachos in the middle of the table.

"Thanks, Crystal," Christina said. Christina's taco was filled with hot ground beef and loaded with lots of diced

Something
To Eat?

Eating &
Thinking

tomatoes, shredded lettuce, melted cheese, and topped with a big glob of sour cream . . . just like she liked it. After taking a big bite, she gulped down a swallow of her pink lemonade, then reached for a gooey nacho.

"Okay . . . so let's take a look at our clues," Mick said, as the girls continued eating. "What did the first voice say, Christina?"

Trying not to talk with her mouth full, Christina quickly chewed up the cheesy nacho in her mouth and took another gulp of her drink.

After wiping a bit of melted cheese off her chin, she said, "First, the voice started singing the Pirates of the Caribbean song."

"Then what did it say?" Crystal asked.

"Well, it told me that if I didn't follow the pirate's rules, it would be the end for me!" Christina continued. "I didn't tell you guys because I thought the message wasn't really for me."

"That's okay, Christina," Crystal said, patting her on the back. "I'm sure it's just a joke or something. We'll find Grant."

"The clues the voice on the boat gave us should help," Mick said. "First, didn't it say something about getting soggy and a rabbit?"

Eating &
Thinking

Going Over
Clues

"Yeah," Christina began. "I guess that's because he had to escape in the water or something."

"But then what was that silly song for?" Crystal asked.

"I know!" Mick said suddenly. "That's the theme song to the old television show *Rawhide!*"

He began to sing the song, *Keep movin', movin', movin', though they're disapprovin', keep them dogies movin', Rawhide!*

Christina couldn't believe that Mick could sing too!

"It's a famous western show from the 1950s and 60s," he explained.

"Wait!" Christina exclaimed. "I know what the clues mean!"

"What? Tell us Christina!" Crystal begged.

"Frontierland!   He's in Frontierland!" Christina shouted.

"Are you sure?" Mick asked.

"Of course . . . it all makes sense now. He's getting soggy on Splash Mountain.   You know, because that's where Brer Bear, Brer Fox, and Brer *Rabbit* are! I bet that's where he is!"

"Well then, what are we waiting for?" Crystal said.

They all stuffed the last few bites of their tacos and

Going Over
Clues

Rawhide!

the nachos into their mouths and chewed as quickly as possible. After a few quick slurps of their drinks, they picked up all their trash and put it into the garbage can next to the door.

"Let's go get Grant!" Christina cheered.

Rawhide!

Off To frontierland

10 SPLISH, SPLASH, DASH!

Christina led Mick and Crystal as they raced out of the restaurant. They crossed over a bridge that took them right to Splash Mountain. Across from the ride, Christina could see Grant's favorite ride, the Big Thunder Mountain Railroad.

The towering pillars of red rock mimicked those Christina had seen out in the desert at the Grand Canyon. Mimi told her that many different kinds of rocks including shale, sandstone, and limestone made formations like these all over the world. Christina wished Grant was with her right now so they could ride the Big Thunder Mountain Railroad together.

When they ran up to Splash Mountain there was another long line weaving in and out of oak trees. Pictures of Brer Bear, Brer Fox, and Brer Rabbit were placed along

Off To
frontierland

Splash
Mountain

the line.

"Thank goodness for our special Fastpasses," Mick said, as they worked their way to the front of the never-ending line. "This will help us find Grant in no time."

"Grant!" Christina cried. "Grant!"

"Hey little buddy, are you here?" Mick asked. She could tell Grant liked Mick because he let Mick call him *little buddy*. Grant never liked any of the nicknames Christina gave him, she thought. But then again, none of them were that nice!

"Grant!" Mick called again.

"Come on you guys," Crystal said, as she waved at them to hurry up. "It's our turn to go on the ride. Maybe he's inside!"

The hollowed-out log boat for this ride had room for two people to sit next to each other. Before they sat down Mick told them, "Make sure you look out for Grant. He could be anywhere on the ride."

Mick let Christina sit down first, and then he sat down next to her. Crystal sat one row back with someone else who wanted to ride.

The boat made a grumbling noise as it launched itself off the track and splashed down into the water. This ride moved much faster then the pirate ride. It made

Splash
Mountain

Looking for
Grant

Christina feel like she was in a cartoon as she passed the colorful scenes of the whole Brer gang. They even splashed over three small waterfalls.

"I'll look to the right if you'll look to the left, okay Christina?" Mick asked.

"Okay. Just look extra hard. Mimi will be so upset if she finds out I've lost Grant!" Christina said. As they continued, she remembered the story behind the ride.

"Can you believe these stories have been around since slavery?" Christina asked Mick.

"What do you mean?" he asked.

"Brer Rabbit is the hero of the *Uncle Remus* stories by Joel Chandler Harris," Christina explained. "Back in the Old South, slaves told these folktales."

"Really? I had no idea," Mick said. "I just thought this ride was after the Disney movie *Song of the South*."

"They're based on the storytelling traditions of West Africa," Christina elaborated. "Brer Rabbit symbolizes a slave who uses wit to overcome his circumstances and take playful revenge on his enemies, who represent the white slave-owners."

"Wow!" Mick said in amazement. "Even *I* didn't know that. You are an expert, aren't you?"

Christina began to blush from Mick's compliment.

Looking for
Grant

Brer Rabbit
& friends

She liked that she impressed him.

"Well, I . . ." she began.

But before she could finish, their boat began chugging its way up a steep hill. When it reached the top, the boat paused for a second, and then began to fall straight down a five-story chute at a 45-degree angle!

"Ahhhhhhhhhhhhhh!" everyone in the boat screamed in unison. Then they landed with a huge splash! The wave of water drenched everyone on the boat.

Christina wiped the water—and her hair—from her face as they passed the final scene of the ride. All of Brer Rabbit's friends were singing "Zip A Dee Doo Dah" while they danced and sang on top of a riverboat.

"Did you know that this riverboat is the largest prop ever used in a Disney ride?" Mick asked Christina.

"Wow! I believe that. It's so huge!" Christina marveled.

"All of Brer Rabbit's friends on the boat were originally built for the America Sings attraction at Disneyland," Mick added.

As they pulled into the unloading station at the end of the ride, Mick helped Christina out of the boat and the two waited for Crystal.

"I didn't see anything," Crystal began. "Did you

Brer Rabbit
& Friends

We Saw
Nothing

guys?"

"No," Christina said. "I don't understand. All the clues led right to this ride."

Just as Christina stopped talking, her walkie-talkie made the static sound again.

"Wait!" Mick cried. "Your walkie-talkie is making noise. I think we're about to get another clue!"

We Saw Nothing

Another Clue?

11 A LITTLE PIECE OF AMERICA

Give me liberty or give me death! the voice said.

"What is he talking about?" Crystal asked worriedly.

"Wait!" Mick said. The voice came back on the walkie-talkie and began to hum the tune to *Hail to the Chief*.

"I knew it!" Mick said. "It's a clue."

10-4, over and out! the voice said, as the walkie-talkie faded to static.

"Yeah," Crystal agreed. "But what does it mean? I know that song from somewhere, but I can't remember where."

"It's *Hail to the Chief*, silly!" Mick said.

"What's that?" Crystal asked.

"The song you always hear when the President of

Another
Clue?

Hail To The
Chief

the United States makes an appearance," Christina answered.

"Okay." Crystal said. "But what's it mean?"

"It means we're going to Liberty Square," Mick answered. "That's where we need to go."

Christina and Crystal trusted Mick and took off running from Frontierland to head toward Liberty Square. They scooted over the wooden bridge and passed by Tom Sawyer's Island. Christina loved *The Adventures of Huckleberry Finn* by Mark Twain. She wished they had time to ride the river raft.

When they came into Liberty Square, Christina noticed how old-fashioned all the buildings looked. "These look like they are right out of a village built during colonial America," Christina said.

"See the street numbers on the buildings?" Mick said. "Those are actually the dates from when the architecture of the building was popular."

"Wow!" Christina said.

The next thing they saw was the replica of the Liberty Bell.

"This looks just like the one we saw in Philadelphia," Crystal said.

"I've always wondered why the Liberty Bell was so

Hail To The
Chief

To Liberty
Square

famous," Mick said.

"We learned about it in school," Christina began. "It's famous because it chimed on July 8, 1776 from the tower of Independence Hall in Philadelphia to summon people to listen to the first public reading of the Declaration of Independence."

"That's cool," Mick said.

"A little more than a year later," Christina explained, "the patriots had to hide the bell in a church basement when the British occupied Philadelphia."

"Were they afraid the British were going to steal the bell?" Crystal asked.

"Actually all the bells in Philadelphia were hidden because they believed that the British would most likely melt them down and make cannon balls," Christina said.

"But where did the cr-cr-crack come from?" Mick wondered.

"A lot of people disagree about when the first crack appeared," Christina explained. "But everyone agrees that the final expansion of the original crack that made the bell cease to ring occurred on George Washington's birthday in 1846."

"How big is the crack?" Crystal asked.

"They say it is half an inch wide and 24 and a half

To Liberty
Square

Liberty Bell
History

inches long," Christina explained. "The real Liberty Bell in Philadelphia is made mostly out of copper. But there are ten different kinds of metal in the bell including tin, lead, and iron. I read that it weighs 2,080 pounds!"

"Hey you guys, don't forget about Grant!" Mick reminded them.

"You're right," Christina said. "Let's go find him."

Right next to the Liberty Bell and in front of the Hall of Presidents, Christina saw the Liberty Tree.

"Did you know that this tree is more than 130 years old, Christina?" Crystal asked.

"Really?" Christina marveled, as she looked up at the giant live oak tree.

"It was discovered on the southern end of the Disney property, and they moved it here," Crystal explained.

"I heard they had to drill two-inch holes into the trunk and put in steel dowel pins to move the 38-ton tree," Mick added.

"Really?" Christina asked in amazement. "But, I don't see any holes."

"That's because once the tree was planted here, they removed the steel pins and replaced them with sections of oak hardwood," Mick explained.

Liberty Bell History

Liberty Tree

"Check it out," Crystal said. "If you look really closely, you can still see where the holes were."

"Wow!" Christina said. "But what are those lanterns hanging in the tree for?"

"Each lantern represents one of the 13 original colonies," Mick explained. "Hey look! We're right on time for the next show at the Hall of Presidents. That's where the clue was leading us."

"I think you're right!" Christina exclaimed. "Let's go inside."

"This is my favorite part of Walt Disney World," Mick told Christina.

"Really? Why is that?" she asked.

"Well, besides the fact that history is my favorite subject, there are so many *cool* things about the Hall of Presidents," Mick explained, as they walked into the hall.

"Like right here," he said, as he pointed to a small, worn marble step.

"What's that?" Christina asked.

"That's actually a step from *Monticello*—Thomas Jefferson's house in Virginia," Mick answered.

"I like it because it's air-conditioned," Crystal explained. "Last time I was here, I took a great nap!"

"Crystal!" Mick admonished. "That is so wrong!

Liberty Tree

Hall Of Presidents

This really is the most fascinating attraction at Disney World if you just pay attention. Come on!"

Mick led them into the 700-seat theater.

"Let's sit up close," he said. Christina could see how excited he was about the show.

As the show began, the narrator's voice seemed familiar to Christina.

"Who's that?" she asked Mick.

"Dr. Maya Angelou," Mick explained. Maya Angelou was one of Christina's favorite poets. Anyone who has been nominated for both a Pulitzer Prize and National Book Award is okay in her book, she thought.

"Did you know that all 42 Presidents are represented up there?" Mick said, as the screen pulled back to reveal the audio-animatronic figures.

"Forty-two?" Christina asked. "But George W. Bush is the 43rd president. Has he not been added yet?"

"He's there," Mick said, as he gestured toward him. "But Grover Cleveland was both the 22nd and 24th President."

Christina watched in amazement as she listened to Maya Angelou introduce each of the Presidents on stage. Each one of the audio-animatronic presidents moved in different ways. Some nodded their heads, while others

Hall Of
Presidents

Moving
Presidents

Brothers!

fidgeted in their seats.

"This attraction is actually a direct descendant of *Great Moments with Mr. Lincoln,* which was first seen at the New York World's Fair in 1964," Mick explained. "The Abe Lincoln you see here was reprogrammed in 1984 and still works today."

"Our Dad always gets aggravated because Mr. Lincoln breaks down from time to time," Crystal giggled. "He's spent many late nights repairing him."

"All of the costumes worn by the Presidents are made from period fabrics," Mick explained. "Some were specially made for the show, and some were donated. President Clinton donated his watch, and Mrs. Carter even comes in and changes President Jimmy Carter's suit from time to time."

"Hey look," Christina said. "There's Harry S. Truman."

"Did you know that he refused to ride the Dumbo ride at Disneyland because the elephant is a Republican symbol and he was a Democrat?" Mick asked.

"Wow," Christina said. "There really is a whole lot about this place that I don't know."

When the audio-animatronic President George W. Bush began to talk, Christina thought he sounded just like

Moving
Presidents

George
Talks!

the real president.

"Is that really him speaking?" she speculated.

"Yes, it is," Mick answered. "He and President Clinton are the only two Presidents who actually recorded their speeches. The others are performed by actors."

If the Declaration of Independence is not the truth, let us get the statue book in which we find it and tear it out . . . the audio-animatronic Abe Lincoln finished.

"I can't get over how real all of the Presidents look when they move," Christina said, as they walked out of the auditorium.

"But I didn't see Grant anywhere!" Crystal exclaimed.

"Shhhhhh!" Mick insisted, as the walkie-talkie began to buzz with static. "I think we're about to get another clue!"

Mick took the walkie-talkie from Christina and held his ear up to its speaker. They all waited patiently until they heard a loud . . .

George Talks!

Walkie Talkie . . .

12 MAKE ROOM FOR ONE MORE

... *BOO!*

"Ahhhhhhhh!"

Mick, Crystal, and Christina screamed in unison as they jumped back. It scared Mick so badly that he dropped the walkie-talkie.

"Oh no!" he cried. "Did I break it?"

"Shhhhh!" Christina answered, as she picked it up off the ground. "No. This thing is almost unbreakable. Now hush! There should be more to the clue."

They waited patiently for the voice. *There's always room for one more!* the voice said. *Mu ah ha ha ha* it chuckled with a ghoulish laugh. *10-4, over and out . . . for now!*

Christina, Mick, and Crystal stared at each other with puzzled looks on their faces.

Walkie Talkie  BOO!

77

"What does that mean?" Christina asked.

"He's just trying to scare you, Christina," Mick said to comfort her. "That wasn't a clue."

"Yes! I think it was," Crystal contradicted. "The Haunted Mansion. That's what he was talking about."

"Are you sure?" Christina asked. "I've never been on that ride."

"Of course!" Mick exclaimed. "'*There's always room for one more*' is said on that ride. That's got to be it!"

"Okay, then. Let's go!" Crystal shouted. Again, she grabbed Christina's hand and pulled her to the next ride.

As they ran up to the mansion, Christina let go of Crystal's hand and paused for a moment.

"What's the matter, Christina?" Crystal asked.

"I can't go in there," she said, with a shiver.

"What do you mean? You know we don't have to wait in line," Crystal answered. "Come on!" She grabbed Christina's hand again and pulled. But Christina did not budge.

"Wait, Crystal," Mick said to his younger sister. "I think I know what it is." He turned to Christina and put his hands on her shoulders.

"You said you've never been on this ride before, right?" he asked compassionately.

BOO!

The Haunted Mansion

"No," she stuttered. "I mean, yes. I mean, I haven't ever."

"It's alright," he said. "It's not as scary as it looks." Christina knew he could see the fear in her eyes. "I'll hold your hand on the ride. That way you won't be too scared."

Christina paused for a moment, holding on to the meandering wrought iron fence leading up to the mansion. She gazed at the frightening 19th century brick home. She saw the glass solarium and the weather vane on top of the copper roof. The mansion looked larger than life as she contemplated going in.

"Alright!" she finally squealed, more bravely than she felt. "Let's go find Grant."

Mick grabbed Christina's hand, and they followed Crystal onto the ride. When they approached the front of the line, the hosts were speaking in low, creepy voices. They looked like characters from a horror movie, Christina thought. She squeezed Mick's hand a little tighter.

"Please drag your bodies to the dead center of the floor," a ghoulish voice directed. The hair on the back of Christina's neck stood up like little spider legs.

Everyone gathered into the middle of the room as the walls began to stretch down revealing a few funny pictures. Christina's whole body was covered with

The Haunted Mansion

Creeped-Out Christina

goosebumps. She thought how scared Grant would be on this ride by himself.

"Don't worry Christina," Mick reassured her, "The walls are actually moving up, we aren't moving down."

They then moved to the boarding area where they took their seats on the Doom Buggies. Mick held on tightly to Christina's hand.

They rode the buggies down hallways, past door knockers that knocked themselves, busts that followed them, and a live suit of armor as a spine-tingling voice guided them along.

Soon they entered a room with a crystal ball. Inside the crystal ball, a head was calling all the ghosts to appear. The buggy began to climb a staircase, where below—in the grand dining room—Christina could see ghosts dancing.

After passing though a dusty old attic and outside into a graveyard, past a bewitching opera singer, Christina thought to herself that it wasn't as bad as she had thought it would be. But then the creepy narrator reminded them to look out for hitchhikers, saying "Don't forget . . . there's always room for one more!"

Christina peered at a mirror in front of her and holding her hand—instead of Mick—was a ghoulish character laughing an awful laugh!

Creeped-Out
Christina

Always Room
for One More

"Ahhhhhhhhhhhh!" she screamed and dropped its hand immediately. When the ride came to a stop, Christina jumped out and ran straight for the exit.

"Christina!" Mick shouted after her. "Wait for me!" Mick ran after Christina out through the exit doors back into the blinding sunlight.

Christina was standing next to the fence trying to catch her breath when she felt a hand on her shoulder.

"Ahhhhhh!" she screamed again. The crowd milling around gave her funny looks.

"What's the matter?" Mick said, as he turned her around with his hand.

"I thought you were . . . I didn't know that . . . I thought it . . ." she stammered, as she tried to catch her breath.

"Hold on, hold on, hold on now!" Mick said, trying to comfort Christina. "Slow down for just a minute, and tell me what's wrong."

Christina paused for a minute to catch her breath. When she regained her composure she looked at Mick.

"When I was on the ride," she began, "the voice said *There's always room for one more!* And that was the clue we were given to find Grant. But when I looked over, you were gone. And sitting next to me—holding my hand—was a

Always Room
for One More

Not A Real
Ghost

ghost!"

"Oh, Christina!" Mick said, as he gave her a hug. "That wasn't a real ghost! That was part of the ride. They use holograms and mirrors to make those ghosts."

"Are you sure?" she asked.

"Yes, I'm sure," he assured her.

"But it looked so real!" she shrieked.

"My Dad will be so glad to hear that," Mick said, proudly.

Christina was confused.

"What do you mean?" she inquired.

"Well, Dad is one of the Imagineers who works on this ride. Our grandfather was one of the original creators. That's why Crystal and I say it's our favorite."

"Speaking of Crystal," Christina said, "where is she? Shouldn't she be off the ride by now?"

"You're right," Mick said, with an alarmed look on his face. "Now Crystal's missing!"

Not A Real
Ghost

Crystal Is
Missing!

13 AROUND THE WORLD

"I don't understand how this could be happening!" Mick roared. "Crystal practically lives here at Walt Disney World. It's just not possible!"

"Now what do we do?" Christina cried. "Grant's missing, and now so is Crystal! I just don't know . . ." But before Christina could finish, her walkie-talkie began to make the static noise again.

Take a trip around the world, the voice said.

"Listen," Christina cried. "The voice is back."

It's a world of laughter, a world of tears. It's a world of hopes and a world of FEARS! the voice sang.

"That's from the theme song for the *It's A Small World* ride," Christina shouted.

"Come on," Mick said. "It's right around the corner. Christina ran as quickly as she could to keep up with Mick

Crystal Is Missing!

Let's Go!

as they left Liberty Square, and headed into Fantasyland.

"It's right there!" Mick shouted, as they saw the tall red, white, and blue canopies reaching high above the building that housed the *It's A Small World* ride. It looked like a little castle with its steep peaks and grand arches. Mick handed Christina their Fastpass, and she flashed it at the ticket man.

"I love this one," Christina said. "The song always gets stuck in my head." They sat down in the small, colorful boat and made their way into the hall. Slowly they drifted through topiary gardens and passed towering columns.

"Look!" Christina said excitedly. "There are the Scandinavian kids!"

"Here comes Europe!" Mick said, as they slowly sailed past England and the London Bridge. Fur-capped Cossacks danced the knee-straining *Gopak*.

"I always thought that looked like fun!" Mick added.

"Look at the magic carpets," Christina said, as they entered Asia. A snake charmer played along with the *It's A Small World* music.

"I want to be a snake charmer, too!" Christina said, as they passed the exotic-looking dancers.

"Wave good-bye to the girls wearing the kimonos!"

Let's Go!

It's A Small World

Mick said, as they left the Asian continent.

"This must be Africa," Christina said, as they passed Cleopatra in an Egyptian Palace.

"Look!" Mick said. "There's a camel! Don't get too close. I hear they spit!"

"Ewwwww!" Christina squealed. She watched as their boat slowly passed the burning desert into a jungle. At a leisurely pace, their boat passed the peaks of the Andes Mountains crowned with llamas.

"Hold on tight," Mick told Christina. "Here's the best part!" Their boat drifted toward the blazing Mayan sun and fire-peaked volcanoes.

"Look," Christina said. "The color of the water is the same color as a turquoise necklace Mimi gave me." The wild fire-dancers of Tahiti and the drifting Polynesian outriggers made Christina want to go to the South Pacific.

As the ride pulled up to the unloading dock, Christina smiled.

"That ride always makes me so happy!" she said.

"I know what you mean," Mick added. "It really makes you think about how different, but at the same time how much alike, everyone in the world is. We all share one moon and one sun, and no matter how far it may seem to get from one place to another, we are really next-door

It's A Small
World

Spitting
Camels

neighbors."

But before Christina could agree, her walkie-talkie began to rattle with static.

"Another clue!" she cried out.

Round and round you go. Where you stop, only I know! the voice chanted.

"What does that mean?" Mick asked Christina.

"I don't know. There's got to be more to it."

Happy birthday to you. . . happy birthday to you. . . 10-4, over and out! the voice finished. And then there was static again.

"This is really getting weird," Christina said. "It's not my birthday, or Grant's. Is it your birthday or Crystal's?"

"No," Mick said. "But . . . it is my un-birthday!"

"Your what?" Christina questioned.

"You know, like in *Alice in Wonderland*. It's my un—birthday," Mick answered.

"Well, what does that have to do with anything?" Christina asked.

"The clues!" Mick explained. "Round and round you go and the birthday song . . . the Mad Tea Party Ride. That's got to be it."

"You're right," Christina exclaimed. "Let's go!"

Another Clue!

Happy
Birthday?

Mick and Christina took off through Fantasyland. As they passed Cinderella's Golden Carrousel, Mick told Christina, "There are 90 hand-painted horses on that ride, and no two are alike."

"I heard it's one of the largest carousels in the world," Christina said. "Mimi told me it wasn't made for Disney World, originally. Someone discovered it at an old amusement park in New Jersey. And since it was built in 1917, they had to totally refurbish it!"

"You do know your Disney, don't you?" Mick said with a smile.

There was a choir of kids, that Christina thought looked about her age singing next to the Dumbo ride. They must be part of the Magic Music Days, she thought to herself.

As they wove their way in and out of the crowd listening to the choir, Christina tried her best to keep up with Mick. When she finally came to a clearing in the crowd, she stopped to search for Mick.

Christina spotted him standing next to Mrs. Potts' Cupboard.

"What are you doing?" she asked.

"I was thirsty!" he said. "And I thought you might be too." The woman behind the counter handed him two

Happy Birthday?

Mrs. Potts' Cupboard

large floats. He unwrapped a straw and dropped it into the creamy mix of soda and ice cream.

"Mmmmmm," Christina said. "My favorite." Quickly Mick and Christina downed their delicious treat.

"That really hit the spot!" Mick said, as he wiped his mouth with a napkin. "Let's go!"

Christina and Mick ran from Mrs. Potts' Cupboard over to the Mad Tea Party ride. There was a long line wrapped around a circular building that looked like a giant circus tent. Inside she could see the pastel pink, blue, and green teacups painted with stars, squiggles, and other fun decorations all spinning around a giant pink teapot—home to a doormouse—in the middle of the ride. She could see moms and dads, brothers and sisters, friends and families all laughing and smiling as they spun around and around in their teacups.

"Look for Grant and Crystal," Mick said. "They could be anywhere."

Christina remembered that the last time Grant rode the Mad Tea Party ride, he was walking in circles afterwards.

"Grant got so dizzy the last time he rode this ride," she recalled.

"That's because the teacups spin out of control

Mrs. Potts'
Cupboard

Mad Tea
Party

around the giant teapot," Mick said. "The reason the teacups spin like that is because one large turntable spins all the teacups in one direction and three smaller turntables spin in the other direction."

Before Mick could continue, Grant's walkie-talkie crackled again.

"Wait," Mick said, "I think we're getting another clue."

Only the mouse knows where to go! the voice said. Then it began to sing, *M I C - K E Y - M O U S E!*

"What?" Christina asked.

10-4, over and out! it said before it faded to static.

"Well that's no help!" Christina cried. "Everything around here is Mickey Mouse."

"Yeah," Mick said, "but we're really close to Mickey's Country House. Maybe they're there?"

"But how do you know that Mickey's House is the answer?" Christina asked. "Mickey is everywhere! There are statues, topiaries, pictures, carvings, paintings, and all other kinds of Mickeys every time you turn around."

"Because he said *only the mouse knows*," Mick answered. "And that's where we can ask him!"

"To Mickey's Toontown Fair it is then!" Christina shouted.

Another Clue?

Mickey Mouse

14 ASK MICKEY!

It was a short hike from the Mad Tea Party to Mickey's Toontown Fair. Christina could tell why little kids really liked this part of the park. It was arranged like an old-timey country fair with big tents and colorful buildings that looked like they were taken straight out of a cartoon with their exaggerated sizes and crazy designs.

"Wait!" Mick stopped and said. "I have an idea. I think maybe we should split up."

"Do what?" Christina said. She was shocked by the idea.

"Well, the voice said *only the mouse knows where to go*, right?" Mick said. "But he didn't say *which* mouse! He could mean Minnie or Mickey."

"Good point!" Christina agreed.

"So I'll go to Minnie's Country House and you go to

Mickey Mouse

Mouse Houses

Mickey's Country House. We can cover more ground that way," Mick explained. "Keep my Fastpass so you can get through the line faster, and let's meet back here in front of Goofy's Wiseacres Farm in 20 minutes. That should give us plenty of time."

"Okay," Christina agreed. But deep down inside, she didn't really feel like going separate ways was the best idea.

Mick headed into the life-size bright bubblegum pink and purple house of Minnie Mouse. Christina thought its exaggerated shape looked like a strange fairytale land. The flagstone chimney was accented with more pink, and cute little hearts adorned everything, including window boxes, shutters, and window peaks.

Christina ran past the manicured hedges in front of Minnie's house and passed the yellow picket fence in front of Mickey's life-size storybook house. Mickey's house was sunshine yellow with a terra-cotta red tile roof. The pillars at the front archway looked like enormous genie bottles.

Once inside, Christina saw Mickey's judge outfit, neatly pressed and hung on the coat rack. Mickey was head judge for the county fair. She passed through the living room where Mickey's overstuffed red chair sat next to an old-fashioned television. In Mickey's office, a picture of

Mouse Houses

Mickey's
House

Let's split up-it will be faster!

Walt Disney in a gold frame—adorned with Mickey Mouse ears—hung above the oversized desk.

Christina giggled at Mickey's kitchen. It seemed as if Donald Duck and Goofy had unsuccessfully attempted to remodel the room with all the mess and clutter everywhere! Then she walked into Mickey's bedroom which had blue and white striped wallpaper. Laid out on the oversized oak bed, with an "M" carved on the footboard, were Mickey's red and white striped pajamas.

Mickey's garden of amusing plants included giant tomatoes adorned with their own "Mickey Ears." Christina saw Pluto's doghouse perched under a tree in the backyard. Like Mickey's house, Pluto's doghouse was sunshine yellow with a red roof.

Christina flashed her pass at the man standing near the Judge's Tent at the rear of Mickey's House. She was immediately moved to the front to meet the most famous rodent in the world. Christina loved Mickey's great big ears and his smile that stretched from ear to ear. She waited as Mickey finished signing an autograph book for a little boy in front of her.

When it was her turn, Christina tugged on Mickey's white gloved hand and whispered, "I need your help!"

Mickey leaned down and cupped his enormous

Mickey's House

Talking To Mickey

white-gloved hand behind his ear to listen.

"Somebody kidnapped my little brother Grant and my friend Crystal!" she told him.

Mickey stood up and slapped both his hands over his mouth in surprise.

"And someone told me that you might know where they are," Christina added.

Mickey put his hands on his hips, and slowly shook his big head back and forth.

"Are you sure?" Christina asked.

Mickey shook his head up and down.

"Well," Christina said dejectedly, "thanks for your help."

Mickey bent down and gave Christina a kiss on top of the head.

"What am I going to do?" she said aloud to no one, as she turned and walked away. "I sure hope Mick had better luck with Minnie."

She glanced at her Carole Marsh Mysteries watch and realized it had been 25 minutes since she left Mick. She was five minutes late!

When she got to their meeting place in front of Goofy's Wiseacres Farm, she didn't see Mick anywhere. She thought to herself that she would wait five more

Talking To
Mickey

No Mick?

minutes. But five minutes went by, then ten. Before she knew it, a half-hour had passed, and still no sign of Mick.

Now Christina was all alone. She was about to cry when her walkie-talkie sputtered. The static was really loud this time.

Dare to go where no man has gone before, it said. Then all of the sudden, the voice started humming the tune to *Star Wars.*

"Who is this?!" Christina screamed into the walkie-talkie. "I want Grant, Crystal, and Mick back now!"

But don't be too terrified. 10-4, over and out! the voice said. The walkie-talkie crackled once more and then was silent.

Christina wasn't sure what she should do. She didn't want Mimi and Papa to know that Grant had been kidnapped, so she couldn't tell them. And she didn't have Crystal or Mick to guide her any more or help her figure out the clues. Christina realized that if she was going to save the day, she had to do it all by herself.

"Okay, think, think, think," she said aloud. "Where have we been?" Christina reached in her pocket and pulled out the map of the park.

"First we went to Adventureland," she said, as she traced her finger along their path. "And then Frontierland.

No Mick?

Another Clue

Next we headed to Liberty Square and then to Fantasyland." She paused for a second. "And now I'm here at Mickey's Toontown Fair." She stopped to remember what her last clue was.

"Of course!" she cheered, as she jumped off the curb. People passing by looked at her like she was crazy. "The only land I haven't been to is Tomorrowland. And all that talk about 'going where no man has gone before' and the theme song to *Star Wars* has to do with outer space! Space Mountain must be where they are!"

Another Clue

Tomorrowland

15 A Trip to Outer Space

Christina quickly folded her map and stuffed it into the back pocket of her flowery skirt. With all that was going on, she had forgotten how much she wanted to ride Space Mountain. Christina had done a report in school about Space Mountain and felt like she knew everything there was to know about the ride.

She raced past the Mad Tea Party and the Tomorrowland Indy Speedway. The last time she and Grant were at Disney, they had raced in Indy cars. She won, of course!

As she looked up high, she saw the Tomorrowland Transit Authority—an elevated transportation system—passing by over her head. Soon she saw the futuristic white dome of Space Mountain come into view.

Christina remembered that the enormous dome was

Tomorrowland

To Space Mountain

180 feet tall and 300 feet around, and was designed by Disney Imagineers. It took 10 years to develop the ride, and two years to build.

As she hurried past the long line, Christina called out the names of her missing friends. "Grant? Mick? Crystal? Are you guys here?" She looked left and right, but the corridors were so dark that she couldn't see anyone.

When she got to the loading dock, she hopped in the front seat of a three-seater rocket. Her favorite part was being in the dark during the whole ride—except for a few twinkling stars and comets in the distance.

Christina held tight as the rocket began to creep up a steep hill until she was blasted "up, up, and away!" as Grant would say.

The thrilling roller coaster soared through outer space for over two minutes. She remembered that the ride only went about 28 miles per hour. But the twists and turns in the dark make it feel like she was going so much faster! And as soon as she began to love the ride even more, it came to a stop. One by one the riders got out of the spaceship and headed back outside.

Christina followed riders into the Tomorrowland Arcade. She hated to pass up her favorite high-tech game—Dance Revolution—where players moved and grooved to

To Space
Mountain

Tomorrowland
Arcade

music by stepping on arrows as they scrolled up a screen. She hoped to find Grant at one of the video games where people could ride a jet ski, a motorcycle, or a snowboard. But he was not there. And she didn't recognized anyone at the low-tech games, like skeeball and air hockey.

Discouraged, Christina pulled out her map and focused on Tomorrowland. She just knew the clue meant they were there somewhere.

She read the names on the list of the different attractions in Tomorrowland. "The Indy Speedway, the Transit Authority, the arcade, Space Mountain . . ."

"Ah-ha!" Christina shouted, as she came to the last name and realized what she had missed. "The Extra*TERROR*estrial Alien Encounter. I forgot the voice said 'not to be *terrified.*' That's got to be it!" She dashed out of the arcade, hoping it wasn't too late to find them.

Christina wiggled her way through the thick crowd past the Merchant of Venus store where you could buy Disney World souvenirs like snow globes, stuffed Disney characters, and jewelry shaped like Mickey Mouse. Mimi had told her that the *Merchant of Venice* was a play written by William Shakespeare, and that the name of the store was a funny version of that title.

At the ExtraTERRORestrial Alien Encounter,

Tomorrowland
Arcade

To The Alien
Encounter

Christina and the other people were led through two large doors into the Interplanetary Convention Centre.

Christina flashed her Fastpass and entered a room where several television screens were mounted high above the crowd. A video told the audience about a mysterious alien corporation named XS-Tech. They demonstrated some new high-tech products—one of which was their teleportation unit.

Christina desperately scanned the crowd for Grant, Mick, or Crystal, when suddenly the doors opened wide into another room. She didn't see the kids anywhere, but kept following the guides who led them in to see a robot named S.I.R.

S.I.R. explained that teleportation involved dematerializing an object at one point, and sending the object's precise atomic configuration to another location. It was then reconstructed at a different location.

S.I.R. demonstrated the process by sending a cute little alien named Skippy from one side of the room to the other. Poor Skippy, Christina thought. When he was teleported to the other side of the room, he was covered in soot and ash.

Suddenly, it hit Christina.

To The Alien
Encounter

Teleported?

"Maybe Grant, Crystal, and Mick were brought here and teleported?" she wondered aloud. But before she could do anything, the crowd was ushered to a large, circular auditorium for the main demonstration of interplanetary teleportation. At the center of the room, stood a massive glass teleporter.

Christina's mind raced trying to think of how she was going to bring her friends back. Shoulder restraints lowered and locked Christina into her seat. Then the lights dimmed, and another set of television screens began to show an XS-Tech employee talking about problems with the teleportation system.

What if they were teleported and never made it? Christina worried. What if they were hurt—or worse—she thought to herself.

The teleporter attempted to teleport the CEO of XS-Tech, Chairman Clench. But instead, something went wrong and a large, loathsome, man-eating alien appeared. Christina screamed along with the rest of the shrieking observers. The XS-Tech technician told the group everything was okay as long as the alien remained behind the teleporter glass.

Christina wished Mick was there to hold her hand on this ride, like he had been there at the Haunted

Teleported?

A Different
Alien!

Mansion. She was sure this was much scarier. But just when she thought the ride might be okay, the lights blinked out and they were plunged into darkness.

"Ahhhhhhhhhhhh!" she screamed in terror. She heard glass break as the alien escaped from the teleporter. The sound of bones crunching and a warm liquid dripping on her arms and legs made Christina scream again.

Christina squinted her eyes and closed them tightly, wishing that the ride were over. Then from behind her, she heard the voice. The same voice from the walkie-talkie! It whispered in her ear, *Never fear my dear, Walt and Mickey are here!*

Christina jumped when she heard the voice. She tried to turn around, but the shoulder restraints wouldn't let her move. Once again, the voice began to sing a familiar tune. *When you wish upon a star, it makes no difference who you are.*

Suddenly, the lights flickered back on and the shoulder restraints lifted. But when Christina turned around, there wasn't anyone sitting in the seat behind her. Puzzled, she stood up and followed the crowd out of the auditorium. *10-4, over and out!* someone behind her said.

Christina spun around, but no one was there.

"Did you hear that?" she asked a boy who walked by.

A Different
Alien!

The Voice
Again

But he didn't answer her.

"Did you hear that?" she asked another person. But she walked right by her without answering.

When Christina walked outside, she saw it was almost dark. She looked at her Carole Marsh Mystery watch and realized it was almost 8:00 p.m.! She only had 30 minutes to find Grant, Crystal, and Mick, and then meet Mimi and Papa. She needed to move quickly!

The Voice Again

Look At The Time!

16 JUST SPELL IT OUT

"The voice said *Never fear, Walt and Mickey are here,*" Christina said aloud. So maybe he's talking about the *Partners* statue of Walt Disney and Mickey Mouse in front of Cinderella's Castle, she thought.

"At this point, I'll try anything!" she said, as she took off running to the center of the Magic Kingdom.

Christina turned a sharp left to leave the ExtraTERRORestrial Alien Encounter and ran under the Tomorrowland main entrance. The futuristic-looking arch definitely looked like something out of a movie that might take place in the year 3003 with its steel arms stretching over the bridge to hold the spinning planet inside.

When she crossed over the bridge and entered the main square, she could see people already claiming their spots for the fireworks show. She carefully wove her way

Look At The Time!

Never Fear

through the dense crowds to reach the *Partners* statue that stood at the end of Main Street USA, on a small circle of grass.

Mimi had told Christina that *Partners* is the hub of the Magic Kingdom beneath Cinderella's Castle. She looked up at the tall bronze statue of Mr. Disney and his lifelong partner Mickey Mouse holding hands, and began to cry.

"I'm never going to find them!" she wailed.

Standing directly in front of the statue, Christina looked up at the creative Walt Disney and asked, "Mr. Disney, what would you do if you were in my situation?" And when the statue didn't answer, Christina knew she needed to go find Mimi and Papa.

Just before she turned around, she saw a light flashing in an upstairs window of Cinderella's Castle. She realized it was Morse code, like she had learned in Girl Scouts.

Christina watched intently as the light flickered on and off. Quick, quick, quick, quick, then pause. Quick, then pause. Quick, long, quick, quick, then pause. Quick, long, long, quick, and then it stopped.

She stopped for a minute to think about what the message meant. "H-E-L-P," Christina spelled out.

Never Fear

Morse Code?

"Someone is asking for help!"

Christina looked back up at the castle, where something else was being communicated. Long, long, quick, then pause.

"G," she said. Quick, long, quick, then pause. "R," she said. Quick, long, then pause. "A," she said. Long, quick, then pause. "N," she said. Long, then pause. "T," she said.

"Grant! It's Grant!" she screamed, partly with joy since she knew where he was, but also from fear for not knowing who was holding him there.

"Don't worry Grant," Christina said. "I'm on my way!"

Morse Code? Grant!

17 THINK LIKE WALT DISNEY

Christina ran as fast as she had ever run before up to Cinderella's 180-foot tall castle. She dashed into the castle, inspired by French 12th and 13th century architecture, to find a way to the top.

Mimi had told her that the outside shell of the castle was made from fiberglass over a steel frame. But the inside walls on the first floor were decorated with elaborate mosaics that depicted the magical Cinderella story.

Christina couldn't help but stop and look at how beautiful the pictures were. She had always been fascinated at how little pieces of stone or glass could be put together to make such an amazing picture. As she looked closely, she could see that the mosaics were adorned with sterling silver and 14-karat gold leaf. She overheard someone say that almost one million tiles in more than 500

Grant!

Cinderella's Castle

shades had created all of the mosaics inside of Cinderella's Castle!

Just as Christina walked by, two security guards came out of a door that said DO NOT ENTER! Christina waited until the guards walked away and the door was almost closed. Then she stopped it with her foot and scooted through the doorway.

Once inside, the castle looked very much like any other building. To her right, there was a door that said SECURITY. To her left, there was a door that said OFFICE. But what most intrigued Christina was the tall staircase that rose up in front of her.

Step by step she climbed the stairs. The steps seemed a little taller than most, and definitely were a lot steeper. She huffed and puffed until she got to the top of the staircase. *Finally*, she thought to herself, breathing hard.

But when she stopped at the top step and turned the corner—she realized there was another set of stairs!

"I can do this," Christina said aloud. "Grant is up there, and I'm going to find him!"

Step by step, Christina worked her way to the top of Cinderella's Castle. She counted a total of 18 stories!

Huffing and puffing, she reached the top of the final

Cinderella's Castle

A Staircase!

staircase, and walked into a large lobby. Everywhere she looked were pictures of Walt Disney and his family members. There were also framed portraits of his famous characters like Mickey Mouse and Donald Duck.

She gazed around as she walked until she reached two large wooden doors. A brass plaque was mounted on one of the doors that said DISNEY FAMILY APARTMENT.

"I didn't know this was here," Christina said to herself.

Suddenly, a large crash came from the other side of the door. Christina jumped back when she heard the noise. Then she heard a blood-curdling scream from inside the apartment.

"Heeeeelp!" the voice cried out. It was Crystal screaming for help.

"Somebody please help us!" another voice bellowed. That must be Mick screaming for help, Christina thought.

"Heeeeelp!" a small voice shrieked. And that was Grant!

Christina didn't know what to do. She could run back downstairs and get one of the security guards, but that would take too long. She knew she didn't have time to run back down 18 flights of stairs, then explain what was happening. And even if they did believe her—which was not

A Staircase!

What To Do?

very likely—they would then have to climb back up all 18 flights of stairs. And so much could happen between now and when they got back, Christina thought anxiously.

Christina knew that if she was going to help her brother and their friends, she was going to have to find a creative solution—*right away!* She looked out a nearby window up into the night sky, and saw a star twinkling in the distance.

"I wish . . ." Christina said. "I wish that I could be like Mr. Disney and use my imagination to solve this problem all by myself!"

And, suddenly—just like magic—Christina snapped her thumb and forefinger together.

"Ah ha!" Christina exclaimed. "I've got it."

What To Do?   I've Got It!

Captive in the castle!

18 THE VOICE

Christina reached for her walkie-talkie. It had been completely silent since she was at Mickey's Toontown Fair. She dialed to different channels and listened to snatches of conversations on the other end.

She started at Channel One, which sounded like another family using walkie-talkies to stay in touch. Then she flipped it to Channel Two and heard nothing but static. But, when she reached Channel Three, Christina found what she wanted.

Christina heard the voices of several different security officers talking to the main security office in Cinderella's Castle.

Castle this is 1-4, do you copy? one voice said.

I read you. Go ahead 1-4, another voice responded.

Castle, I have another missing persons report for you,

I've Got It!

Security Channel

117

the first voice answered.

Another one!? the second said. *Did this one have a picture attached to a character on a ride too?*

Yep. This is my 10ᵗʰ one today, Castle. Have you found any of the other missing kids? the first voice called back.

No sir. That makes 10 reported and 10 unsolved. Over, the second voice replied. *Bring the family to the Castle office. We'll put them with the rest of the parents.*

10-4 Castle, over and out!

Christina knew that she was on the same walkie-talkie channel as the security guards. She had no idea that other kids were missing too. With Grant, Crystal, and Mick missing, that made 13. . . Christina's most despised number!

Christina decided it was now or never. She pushed the button on the side of her walkie-talkie and said, "Castle, do you read me?"

She only heard static at first, but then the same voice came over the line as before. *This is Castle. . . identify yourself, please!*

"My name is Christina. I'm at the top of Cinderella's Castle," Christina answered.

Honey, this is not a toy. You shouldn't be playing on that radio, the voice answered. She knew they weren't

Security
Channel

Castle? This
Is Christina

going to take her seriously.

"You said there are 10 kids missing, right? Well, I know where they are. They are up here in the Disney Family Apartment. And if someone doesn't come quickly, I'm afraid something bad is going to happen to them!" Christina said, as quickly as she could.

I'm sending someone up to come and get you. Please stay where you are, the voice answered.

"I'm sorry, ma'am. But I can't do that. I'm going in to help my little brother. So just send as many people as you can, quickly!" Christina finished. Before the voice could protest, Christina turned her radio's volume all the way down.

"Here I go," Christina said. She reached down and turned the brass doorknob. It wasn't locked, which surprised Christina. Slowly she opened the heavy oak door trying to be as quiet as a mouse. The door began to creak, and so Christina paused for a second. But when she didn't hear anything, she continued to open the door. Once the opening was big enough for her to squeeze through, she cautiously tiptoed into the apartment.

As quietly as she opened the door, Christina closed it behind her. The front foyer of the apartment split in three long hallways going in different directions. Listening

Castle? This Is Christina

Into The Apartment

carefully, Christina heard voices coming from the hallway to the left.

Christina tiptoed over to the door that was barely cracked open. Inside, she could see a man and a woman sitting at a table. On the table there was a deck of playing cards, a couple of soda cans, and a walkie-talkie. She listened carefully to what they were saying.

"Bobby," the man at the table said, "at least one of these kids' families has got to have some money. And besides, we didn't even get to ride the Tea Cups!"

"Give it up already with the Tea Cups, Douglas!" the woman said. "We picked the kids up like you told us to. You know, the ones who were lagging behind their parents. You didn't tell us to find out if their parents were rich or poor as church mice!"

Then another man walked in front of the door where Christina was standing. "Obviously, you didn't listen very well, did you, Lisa? Did you, Douglas? This is one of the busiest weeks of the year at Walt Disney World. All of these kids who are here for the Magical Music Days made this the perfect time to kidnap a rich kid," he said to the others. "But instead, I have 13 screaming kids, and none of them are any good to me. And I've been doing my best to give that little brat with the walkie-talkie the run-around! But I

Into The
Apartment

Kidnappers!

think she's getting closer to finding us," the man said.

But Christina didn't want to stick around to hear any more. She quickly crept back toward the door and followed the hallway to the right. At the end of the hallway there was another door. When she walked up to it, she pushed her ear against it.

"I'm never going to see my mommy again, am I?" a little girl's voice cried.

"Don't worry. I'll help you!" she heard Mick's voice say.

Hanging on a nail by the door was a key chain with several different keys on it. Christina stood on her tiptoes, but her fingertips barely grazed the keys.

Desperately, she looked around the hallway for something she could stand on. On top of a table in the hallway Christina saw several books. She hurried over to the table and picked the two thickest books she could find. Then she walked back over to the door and set the books down on the floor. Slowly, she stepped up onto her makeshift stool, and reached the keys.

"Now, I want to see a rich kid here in this apartment before the fireworks start which is in 30 minutes!" Christina recognized the voice as the one she had heard over the walkie-talkie. "And find that little brat with the

Kidnappers!

Gotta Get
The Keys

walkie-talkie!"

"Do I have time for the Tea Cups?" the other man asked.

"Just go already!" the voice screamed. Christina could hear the door opening in the other hall.

Quickly, Christina jumped down off the books, picked them up, and ran through an open door into another room in the hall. Once inside, Christina ran to the closet and closed the door behind her. She could hear footsteps coming her way!

Gotta Get
The Keys

Time To
Hide!

19 DON'T MAKE A SOUND

Christina heard three sets of footsteps walking down the hallway to the front door. They paused for a moment and she heard voices, though she couldn't quite tell what they were saying. Then Christina heard the front door open and close.

Quickly, Christina opened the closet door and set the books down onto the bed in the room. She headed for the door when she heard footsteps coming down the hallway! She spun around and went back into the closet. She closed the door behind her, but then realized she had left the books on the bed!

The footsteps kept coming closer. She knew she didn't have time to go back out into the room and get them. Christina closed her eyes tightly and wished the man wouldn't notice them.

Time To Hide!

The Books!

Outside of her door, Christina heard the footsteps pause. She held her breath so she would not make a sound. But then she heard footsteps come into the room. As still as a statue, Christina waited for the man to leave. Through the slats in the closet door, she could see it was the man who had told the other two what to do. She thought he must be the ringleader.

The man walked over to the bed and picked up the two books Christina had left there. Christina knew she was caught for sure.

"Douglas! Lisa! What am I going to do with those two? I told them not to move stuff around up here!" the voice said. Then he turned and stomped out of the room.

Christina gasped for air. She didn't remember having ever held her breath for that long. She heard the man walk over to the table. It sounded like he was putting the books back in their place. Then she heard the footsteps moving further and further down the hall. When she heard a door shut, Christina again opened the closet door.

Slowly she walked out of the room she was hiding in and peeked around the corner. Thankfully, she didn't see anyone in the hallway. Christina ran back over to the table and picked up her two books. She turned and placed

The Books!

Whew! That Was Close!

the books underneath where the keys were hanging, and plucked them from their hook.

Quickly, Christina fumbled with the keys in the lock. Please Mr. Disney, she thought to herself, help me pick the right key. When Christina looked down at the keys, she realized that one of the keys had a Mickey Mouse shaped hole in it. This must be it, she thought.

Christina stuck the key into the lock and turned it to the left. Please work, she prayed. All of a sudden she heard a click and the door opened!

All of the kids inside looked suddenly toward the door. Christina could tell they were all very scared by the way that they were huddled together, some crying. She saw Mick sitting with his arm around his sister Crystal and Grant standing with a flashlight pointed out a window.

"Who are you?" one of the other kids said.

"Christina!" Grant shouted.

"Shhhhhhhh! No one knows I'm here. Come on, we need to get out of here quickly," Christina said. "Let's go!"

Christina grabbed Grant's hand, and they led the way through the hallway back to the front door. One by one, each of the kids tiptoed out of the door. She asked Mick and Crystal to wait until all the kids were out of the

Whew! That Was Close!

Lots Of Kids!

room before they followed. Mick was the last kid to get out into the lobby of the apartment. He quietly closed the door behind him.

Just as the door closed, someone burst through the door to the stairwell.

"Ahhhhhhhhhhh!" all the children screamed.

"Disney Security," one of the men dressed in black said. "Are you alright?"

"He's in there," Christina cried.

"In the apartment?" the man asked.

"Yes, and the other two just left a few minutes ago. They were going to kidnap more kids," Christina answered.

"I know young lady. We caught them on our way up. Now which way is he?" asked the security guard urgently.

"Go to the hallway on the left," Christina said. "He's in that first room."

"Got it," the security guard said. "Let's go!"

After one of the other guards helped the children down the 18 flights of stairs, they were led into an office where several sets of anxious parents were waiting. The door to the security office was open. Inside, Christina

Lots Of Kids!

Kidnappers Caught

could see the two kidnappers in handcuffs. The man was crying . . . "I want my mommy!"

Moms, dads, brothers, and sisters alike were so happy to be reunited.

"You're a real hero," Mick said to Christina.

"No I'm not," Christina said shyly. "You would have done the same thing, Mick."

"How'd you do it?" Mick asked.

"Well, I did what Mr. Disney would do!" Christina said.

"What do you mean?" Mick asked.

"I made a wish upon a star. I wished that I would have the imagination to solve my problem," Christina said. "And just like magic, I came up with a plan!"

"Hey, Christina," Grant said, as he grabbed his sister's hand. "Thank you!"

"You're welcome Grant," she said. Then Christina gave Grant a big bear hug. She squeezed him as tightly as she could.

"Hey, Christina," Grant mumbled, "you're cutting off my air supply!"

"Oh, Grant. I'm sorry. I'm just so glad you're safe," Christina said.

Then Grant asked, "So can we go on Big Mountain

Kidnappers
Caught

Everyone Is
Reunited

Railroad Thunder now?"

"Graaaaant!" Mick, Christina, and Crystal moaned together!

A little girl came up to Christina and tapped her on the shoulder.

"Thank you for saving me, ma'am. You're my hero!" she said, blushing.

"You're welcome, but I'm not a hero," Christina said.

"Yes, you are!" one of the security guards said to her.

Then one by one each of the other kids came up to Christina and thanked her. Each of the parents also thanked her as they walked out of the security office and took their children home.

"Where are *your* parents, kids?" the security guard asked.

Christina looked at the clock above the door.

"Mimi and Papa!" she yelped. "We're going to be late!

Everyone Is
Reunited!

We're Going
To Be Late!

20 A LITTLE MAGIC

Christina, Grant, Mick, and Crystal barely made it to the front of the castle in time. Waiting patiently were Mimi, Papa, and Mick and Crystal's Dad.

Christina jumped into Papa's arms as Grant wrapped his entire body around Mimi.

"Well, hello there!" Mimi said. "I take it you two missed us."

"Oh, Mimi," Christina said. "You have no idea how much we missed you!"

"We're sorry we didn't get the chance to call you on those walkie-talkies," Papa said, as he set Christina back down. "We were just so busy with our Imagineer friend here that we just lost track of time. Before we knew it, it was time to meet you back here!"

"You mean you didn't try to call us *at all*?!"

We're Going To Be Late!

Mimi & Papa!

Christina asked.

"We were just so busy. Plus, we knew you were having a good time too. We didn't want to pester you!" Papa said.

Christina, Grant, Mick, and Crystal all looked at each other and then doubled over in riotous laughter! They knew Mimi and Papa didn't have any idea what they had been through.

"Did you find an idea for your mystery, Mimi?" Grant asked.

"Well, I sure learned a lot today," Mimi began. "But, I just can't imagine what I'm going to do for the mystery part of it. However, I'm certain that a good plot will come to me like . . . magic!"

"Oh, don't worry," Christina giggled. "Have we got a mystery for you!"

Arm in arm, Christina, Mick, Grant, and Crystal paraded in front of the grownups back to the *Partners* statue to watch the grand finale fireworks display.

Loud eruptions of bright yellow firecrackers sizzled and spiraling red sparkles filled the night sky. Bright blue bursts and booming blazes painted the sky. The deafening pops made Grant jump every time.

Mick reached over and took Christina's hand.

"A dream is a wish your heart makes, Christina. Or at

Mimi & Papa!

They Never Knew . . .

When you wish upon a star. . .

least that's what I've heard. So what's your dream?" he asked softly.

Christina paused for a minute before answering. "I wish that all the little boys and girls in the world would get the chance to come here to Walt Disney World one day."

"Why is that?" Mick asked.

"I hope that when they are here they will see what a little ingenuity, creativity, and magic that one man—or woman—can create when they imagine the future and work hard to make it come true."

"I agree!" Mick said.

"So do I!" Crystal chimed in.

"Me too!" Grant added.

"Hey!" Papa said, frantically searching his pockets. "Where are our tickets for tomorrow?"

"Paaaaappaaaaa!" they all squealed, as they lay back on the ground and admired the magical sky!

The End

They Never Knew . . .

The Magic Sky

DISNEY

Places To Go & Things To Know!

Walt Disney's Boyhood Home, Marceline, Missouri – Home where Walt and Roy Disney lived and grew up

Missouri State Historic Site, Kansas City, Missouri – First commercial film studio operated by Walt Disney

The Depot Museum, Marceline, Missouri – Museum with exhibits about the lives of Walt and Roy Disney

Walt Disney Municipal Park, Marceline, Missouri – Relocated home from Disneyland

The Walt Disney Studios, Burbank, California – Where all the magic happens!

Disneyland, Anaheim, California – First theme park built by Walt Disney

The Magic Kingdom, Walt Disney World, Orlando, Florida – Main section of park complex, includes Cinderella Castle and six different theme areas

EPCOT Center, Walt Disney World, Orlando, Florida –
Experimental Prototype Community of Tomorrow and World
Showcase

*Disney's Animal Kingdom, Walt Disney World, Orlando,
Florida* – Newest park in Walt Disney World; features The
Oasis, Tree of Life, Discovery Island, DinoLand U.S.A., Asia,
Africa, and Camp Minnie-Mickey

Disney's Blizzard Beach, Walt Disney World, Orlando, Florida –
Where snow and sun meet—a water park unlike any other

Disney MGM Studios, Walt Disney World, Orlando, Florida –
Recreated 1940s movie studios include live shows, stunt
demonstrations, animation attractions; shows how movies and
television shows are made

*Disney's Wide World of Sports Complex, Walt Disney World,
Orlando, Florida* – Facility where professional sports teams
come to practice and play; kids can watch team practices,
amateur events, or even professional games

Disney's Typhoon Lagoon, Walt Disney World, Orlando, Florida –
Waterpark includes an ocean with five-foot waves, raft ride,
water slides, and a Shark Reef where kids can actually swim
with sharks

The Disney Family Museum website,
http://disney.go.com/disneyatoz/waltdisney/home.html
Maintained by the non-profit Walt Disney Family Foundation

Museum of Animation History, www.animationhistory.com –
Features Walt Disney in the Hall of Fame and also Snow White

ABOUT THE AUTHOR

Carole Marsh is an author and publisher who has written many works of fiction and non-fiction for young readers. She travels throughout the United States and around the world to research her books. In 1979 Carole Marsh was named Communicator of the Year for her corporate communications work with major national and international corporations.

Marsh is the founder and CEO of Gallopade International, established in 1979. Today, Gallopade International is widely recognized as a leading source of educational materials for every state and many countries. Marsh and Gallopade were recipients of the 2002 Teachers' Choice Award. Marsh has written more than 50 Carole Marsh Mysteries™. Years ago, her children, Michele and Michael, were the original characters in her mystery books. Today, they continue the Carole Marsh Books tradition by working at Gallopade. By adding grandchildren Grant and Christina as new mystery characters, she has continued the tradition for a third generation.

Ms. Marsh welcomes correspondence from her readers. You can e-mail her at fanclub@gallopade.com, visit the carolemarshmysteries.com website, or write to her in care of Gallopade International, P.O. Box 2779, Peachtree City, Georgia, 30269 USA.

Glossary

creative: the ability to bring new things into being

diligent: careful and steady effort

epiphany: an illuminating discovery

extraordinary: different from what is common or average

imaginative: having or showing the ability to create new ideas

incredible: so great, unusual, or special that it is hard to believe

ingenious: clever or skillful

inspirational: the ability to cause, urge, or influence others to do something

magical: giving a feeling of enchantment

patriotic: showing great love and loyalty for your country

persistent: refusing to give up

spectacular: something unusual or grand

SCAVENGER HUNT!

Recipe for fun: Read the book, visit the place, find the items on this list and check them off! (Hint: Look high and low!!) *Teachers: you have permission to reproduce this form for your students.*

__1. map of Walt Disney World

__2. "Welcome to Walt Disney World" sign

__3. Disney World Employee name tag

__4. Adventureland Sign

__5. the Liberty Tree

__6. a Talking Crystal Ball

__7. a doormouse

__8. Mickey Mouse

__9. a teleportation machine

__10. a wall mosaic

WRITE YOUR OWN MYSTERY!

Make up a dramatic title!

You can pick four real kid characters!

Select a real place for the story's setting!

Try writing your first draft!

Edit your first draft!

Read your final draft aloud!

You can add art, photos or illustrations!

Share your book with others and send me a copy!

Six Secret Writing tips from Carole Marsh!

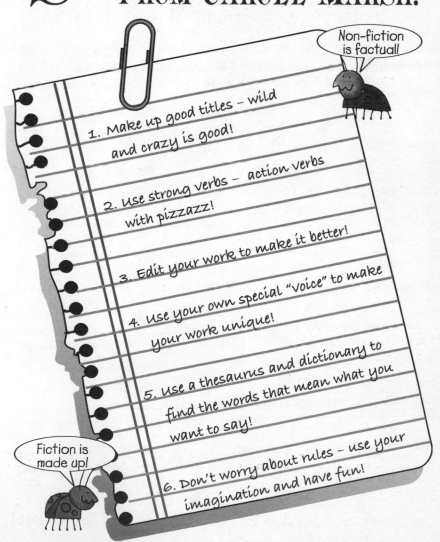

Non-fiction is factual!

1. Make up good titles – wild and crazy is good!

2. Use strong verbs – action verbs with pizzazz!

3. Edit your work to make it better!

4. Use your own special "voice" to make your work unique!

5. Use a thesaurus and dictionary to find the words that mean what you want to say!

Fiction is made up!

6. Don't worry about rules – use your imagination and have fun!

WOULD YOU LIKE TO BE
A CHARACTER IN A CAROLE MARSH MYSTERY?

If you would like to star in a Carole Marsh Mystery, fill out the form below and write a 25-word paragraph about why you think you would make a good character! Once you're done, ask your mom or dad to send this page to:

Carole Marsh Mysteries Fan Club
Gallopade International
P.O. Box 2779
Peachtree City, GA 30269

My name is: _____

I am a: ____boy _____ girl   Age: _____

I live at: _____

City: _____   State:____   Zip code: _____

My e-mail address: _____

My phone number is: _____

_____
_____
_____
_____
_____
_____
_____
_____
_____
_____

Enjoy this exciting excerpt from

THE MYSTERY ON THE UNDERGROUND RAILROAD

1 YOU HAVE MYSTERY MAIL

Christina was doing a stellar job helping her Grandmother Mimi when the intriguing e-mail invitation arrived. Grant was also being a big help by stuffing the giant pile of newspaper clippings, scattered across Mimi's desk, back into the correct color-coded folders.

Christina Yother, 9, a fourth-grader in Peachtree City, Georgia, her brother Grant, 7, and Mimi stood staring at the new message on Mimi's office computer screen. Suddenly, Mimi's 122 unread e-mails were completely forgotten.

Dear Aunt Mimi:
The National Park Service, The National Museum of

American History, Professor William B. Still and I invite
Christina and Grant to ride the *Freedom Road* on the U.R.R.
We'll be pulling into Baltimore next Tuesday to pick up four
passengers. We'll rendezvous with you and the other VIPs in
Philly for the formal ribbon cutting on the Fourth of July.

    Priscilla :-)

    Assistant Curator

    Next Tuesday? The notice was short but Christina
knew that didn't really matter to her Grandmother Mimi. She
was not like most grandmothers. She wasn't really like a
grandmother at all. She had blond hair, wore trendy clothes,
was CEO of her own company, and traveled all around the
country!

    Mimi tapped the message on the screen with her pink
fingernail as she thought about it. "Hmmm," she said. "This
just needs some organization and action, but what an adventure
this could be!" Mimi typed a reply, then reached for her cell
phone.

    Christina was nearly bursting with questions. "Mimi, is
this a good time to ask questions?"

    "You bet!" said Mimi, stroking her granddaughter's
soft, chestnut-colored hair. "I always have time for questions!"

    But Christina shocked her grandmother by reeling out
a string of questions: "Why does the e-mail say National
Museum of American History? Is this the same U.R.R. we
learned about in school? Did Cousin Priscilla get a new job?
Isn't that museum in Washington, DC? What exactly is the

Freedom Road? Does this mean we'll all be together for a Philadelphia Fourth of July celebration? Are you a VIP?"

"Whoa! Good questions!" said Mimi. "Let's start at the end and work our way forward. It's important to remember that everyone we meet is a very important person (VIP) and should be treated with courtesy and respect. Yes, this means we will all be in Philadelphia for the Fourth of July. So much of America's history happened there that it's one of my favorite places to be!"

Mimi took a deep breath and continued answering Christina's many questions. *"Freedom Road* is a new mobile American History museum. Priscilla is still a wonderful fourth grade history teacher and marathoner! She has worked at the museum every summer since she was in high school. Papa and I have been helping with the research for this new museum-on-wheels, so we've been invited to the ribbon-cutting for *Freedom Road's* official Grand Opening."

Mimi paused for another breath and added, "By the way, congratulations on remembering! It *is* the very same U.R.R. you learned about in school.

Mimi looked down at Grant who was still staring at the screen with a perplexed expression. He looked serious. "Everything okay, Grant?" asked Mimi.

Perched on the edge of her office chair, with his legs swinging high above the floor, Grant looked very small. His blue eyes seemed the biggest part of him. He looked up. "Well for one thing, I haven't studied U.R.R. or *urrrr*. Or however you say it! Is it like *grrrr*? I happen to know a lot about *grrrr*.

Grrrr could be a bear or an angry dog. Papa told me that I'm supposed to remain as 'still as a statue' if I hear *that* sound. I still have a question. It might sound dumb, but we haven't covered all the things in my grade that Christina knows."

"What's that?" asked Mimi. "There are no dumb questions, you know."

Grant quietly asked, "Mimi, what *is* U.R.R.?"

His grandmother squeezed his small tense shoulder and smiled. "Grant, that's a wonderful question! It stands for the Underground Railroad. The Underground Railroad didn't have railroad cars or rails. It had people. It was a top secret organization of people, both black and white, who risked their lives to help slaves escape from Southern states, where slavery was allowed, to freedom in the North."

Since Grant still looked confused, Mimi continued her explanation. "Some people say that the Underground Railroad really began in the 1700s when slaves were brought to America from Africa. Other people say it began about 1830 when it got an official name. The railroad was spoken of in hopeful whispers and hidden in songs that were sung across the plantations. The organization had its own secret language, clues, and codes. Even today the story of the slaves' escape to freedom is filled with myths and mystery."

Grant still looked concerned. Mimi asked, "Are you still worried about something?"

Grant looked at this grandmother thoughtfully. "If we're going to be traveling under the ground, will Priscilla bring the flashlights, or should we each bring our own?"